JOHN HAY

THE COMPLETE SHORT STORIES

WINDHAM CRITICAL EDITIONS SERIES

John Hay: The Complete Short Stories
Edited by George Monteiro

JOHN HAY

THE COMPLETE SHORT

STORIES

Edited, with an Introduction by

George Monteiro

BRICKTOP HILL BOOKS

2018

Bricktop Hill Books
PO Box 1016
Willimantic, CT 06226

Library of Congress Control Number: 2018940682

ISBN: 978-0-9973669-4-5

ISBN: 0-9973669-4-x

To Norma Matarissi Kacen

and

To David A. Jonah, *in memoriam*

Contents

TEXTS

John Hay's stories were first published: "Red, White, and Blue," *Harper's Weekly* (Oct. 19, 1861), 5: 666-67; "Shelby Cabell," *Harper's New Monthly Magazine* (Oct., 1866), 33: 601-11; "The Foster-Brothers," *Harper's New Monthly Magazine* (Sept., 1869), 39: 535-44; "Kane and Abel," *Frank Leslie's Illustrated Newspaper* (Apr. 22, 1871), 85-87, and (Apr. 29, 1871), 106-07; and "The Blood Seedling," *Lippincott's Magazine* (Mar., 1871), 7: 281-93. "The Blood Seedling" also appeared in *Prairie Farmer* (Chicago), Mar. 4, 11, and 18, 1871, 42: 70, 78, 86; *Not Pretty, But Precious and Other Stories* (Philadelphia: Lippincott's, 1872), pp. 57-69; *San Francisco Argonaut* (Jan. 5, 1884), 14: 4-6; and *Lippincott's Magazine* (Oct., 1905), 76: 441-57.

An early story, "The Minstrel," dates from the 1850s during John Hay's student days at Brown University. All indications—Hay's handwriting, his signature on the title page ("J. M. Hay"), the story's medieval setting and romantic subject—point to the years preceding Hay's White House days (1861–1865). The manuscript in the John Hay Collection, Brown University Libraries, was not published until 1977: "'The Minstrel': An Unpublished Story by John Hay," ed. George Monteiro, *Books at Brown* (1977), 25: 27-42. The story appears here in the Appendix. The texts used are faithful to the texts as first published. Thus, his spellings and coinages, as well as his notations of speech as he may have heard it are retained.

Introduction

John Hay's Literary Career

John Hay died in office. He was at the time, as he had been since 1898, the U.S. Secretary of State. As Henry Adams declared in *The Education of Henry Adams* (1918), Hay "had solved nearly every old problem of American statesmanship . . . For the first time in fifteen hundred years a true Roman *pax* was in sight, and would, if it succeeded, owe its virtues to him."[1] Under presidents William McKinley and Theodore Roosevelt, Hay had become one of the nation's great heroes.

But John Hay had also been a poet and historian of considerable fame. As William Dean Howells wrote in the *North American Review* in the year of Hay's death, "He lived to be recognized as the ablest public man of his time, the inventor of a diplomacy that was sincere, courageous and generous, and it has seemed to me, in reviewing what he wrote, that he might have had an equal and a kindred fame in literature."[2] At some point Hay had made a choice of public service over literature. And yet, although he had, intermittently at first and then predominantly, chosen the political life of a public servant, in 1904 Hay's literary fame was handsome enough to have him numbered among the very first seven individuals elected to the American Academy of Arts and Letters, and although Howells also numbered among the first seven, Henry James and Henry Adams did not.

John Milton Hay was born on October 8, 1838, in Salem, Indiana, the fourth child of Dr. Charles Hay and Helen Leonard Hay, who were transplanted New

Englanders. Three years later the Hay family, which ultimately included six children, moved to Spunky Point, later called Warsaw, Illinois. Hay was educated in Pittsfield, Illinois, at a private classical school, and later, in 1852-1855, he attended college in Springfield, Illinois. In September 1855, Hay went east, to matriculate at Brown University with advanced standing as a member of the sophomore class. During his stay at Brown (graduating, in June 1858, the class poet), he distinguished himself as much for his poetry as for his studies, meeting in the course of those years the poet Sarah Helen Whitman, once Edgar Allan Poe's fiancée. He formed closer friendships with Nora Perry and Hannah Angell, to both of whom he addressed his poet's letters from Warsaw after his departure from Providence. In a letter to Nora Perry, the young poet wrote in October 1858: "In spite of the praise which you continuously lavish upon the West, I must respectfully assert that I find only a dreary waste of heartless materialism, where great and heroic qualities may indeed bully their way up into the glare, but the flowers of existence invariably droop and wither. So in time I shall change. I shall turn from 'the rose and the rainbow' to corner-lots and tax-titles, and a few years will find my eye not rolling in a fine frenzy, but steadily fixed on the pole-star of humanity, $!"[3]

After some floundering, Hay finally decided to read law in the office of an uncle, Milton Hay, in Springfield, Illinois. There he met John G. Nicolay, who was a clerk in the Illinois secretary of state's office. He also became known to the partners in the law firm of Abraham Lincoln and William Herndon, located next door to his uncle's office. In 1860, when Abraham Lincoln won the Republican nomination and ran for president, Hay campaigned for him both personally and through reports to the *Providence Journal* and the *Missouri Democrat*. Upon Lincoln's election, he and Nicolay were rewarded with appointments as White House secretaries to the president himself. During his tenure in the White House, Hay dispatched his duties with competence, spirit, and intelligence. Despite the pressing duties of assisting a president who was conducting a major civil war, Hay found time to write and publish poetry and essays in periodicals, as well as at least one patriotic story, "Red, White, and Blue," dealing with the duties of those who would be faithful and responsible to the Union. It was published, fittingly, amid engravings of war scenes and national heroes in *Harper's Weekly* in 1861. Early in 1865, with the end of the war imminent, Hay made plans to change careers. Sporting the recently acquired rank of colonel (by which he would be known, off and on, for the rest of his life), Hay secured a consular post in Europe, serving over the next five years initially as first secretary of the United States legation in Paris (1865-1867), then as *charge d'affaires* at Vienna (1867-1868), and finally as secretary of the legation at Madrid (1868-1870).

During this period he continued to write for American journals. He prepared essays on inevitable topics for the American interested in Europe (such as "Down the Danube") and for an America reaching back into the nexus of parochial and national history ("The Mormon Prophet's Tragedy"). He wrote stories drawing upon his Parisian experiences ("Shelby Cabell" and "Kane and Abel") as well as on regional boyhood experiences ("The Foster-Brothers" and "The Blood Seedling"). In the stories set in Paris, Hay emphasizes the early international notion that grave dangers await innocent and not-so-innocent Americans trying to make their way in Paris, while in the Midwestern stories he concerns himself, respectively, with the bitter wages of love and miscegenation and the murderous proclivities in the heart of the Midwestern farmer (the dark side of the Pike County Golyers in his humorous poems). While still a member of the legation at Madrid, he began to write essays about his experiences there that, after his return to the United States in 1870, would become part of *Castilian Days* (1871), which brought him considerable acclaim.

Calling an end to his consular career in 1870, he accepted an offer to write editorials on a daily basis for the *New York Tribune*. In the years he spent with the *Tribune*, he earned the highest praise from the newspaper's senior editor, Horace Greeley, who once called Hay "the best newspaper writer in the United States."[4] Within months of joining the *Tribune*, however, Hay had achieved another kind of fame. In the pages of the *Tribune* were published the first of his regional poems, "Little Breeches" (Nov. 19, 1870) and "Jim Bludso (of the Prairie Belle)" (Jan. 5, 1871). The poems caught on and, like wildfire, spread across the newspapers and journals of the nation.

Dealing with "Western" subjects and featuring the regional dialect of Pike County, the success of these poems encouraged the writing of others, "Banty Tim" and "The Mystery of Gilgal." Their success also made it possible for Hay to establish himself as a poet with the publication of *Pike County Ballads and Other Pieces* (1871), including 16 pages of the ballads and 137 pages of the other kinds of poetry Hay had been writing since his university days.

On February 4, 1874, he married Clara Louise Stone, the daughter of the wealthy Amasa Stone of Cleveland, Ohio. In less than seventeen months, Hay resigned from the *Tribune* and moved to Cleveland to participate in

Amasa Stone's financial affairs. He also assumed an active role in Ohio politics, a role that in 1879 resulted in his appointment as assistant secretary of state by President Rutherford B. Hayes. He served until March 1881, when he agreed to return to New York to edit the *Tribune* for six months while his friend Whitelaw Reid honeymooned in Europe.

Hay's public literary career between the end of his duty with the *Tribune* in 1875 and his return to the paper in 1881 was hardly auspicious. In 1881-1882, however, he wrote anonymous reviews of novels for the *Tribune* (including one of Henry James's *The Portrait of a Lady*) and of various books relating to the Union generals in the Civil War.[5] The latter reviews lead us to Hay's major literary work of this period and of the next decade as well—his researching and writing toward the monumental *Abraham Lincoln: A History*, done in collaboration with his friend and former fellow worker in the White House, John G. Nicolay. Announced intermittently over more than a decade, *Abraham Lincoln* was serialized by the *Century* (which paid the authors $50,000) over the period Nov. 1886—Feb. 1890, before appearing in ten volumes in 1890.

But his work on Lincoln was not Hay's only literary work in the 1880s. In August 1883 appeared the first installment of *The Bread-Winners*, the novel he serialized anonymously in the *Century* through January 1884 before it appeared as a book later that year. An early anti-labor novel reflecting the establishment's alarm over the growing threats to the social, political, and economic status quo exemplified in the violent strikes of 1877 and their fallout, *The Bread-Winners* is a serious, intelligent work marked by a sprightly, engaged style. The novel, like the shorter fiction, also reflects its author's broad racism, class bias, and antisemitism, attitudes he shared with many of his time and place, including his prominent friends, the novelist Henry James and the historian-writer Henry Adams.

Yet John Hay's fiction is worth reading today as a barometer of its times. Consider, for example, his portrait in the *Bread-Winners* of the self-made high-school graduate who brazenly challengers her "betters." Maude Matchin represented a new type of woman, and John Hay was the first to depict that type in a novel. Something of the author's attitude toward such social self-starters, though, is revealed in his not-so-jocular motto, "Love your neighbor, but be careful of your neighborhood."[6]

The Bread-Winners also includes something of a self-portrait of its author in the character Arthur Farnham, who presents Hay's own sense of himself as a member of beleaguered society. Like Farnham, when things public began to upset Hay, he would take himself off to Europe. And for two decades that is exactly what Hay did, as he enjoyed his wife's wealth, indulged his hypochondria, and cultivated friends and acquaintances on both sides of the Atlantic. And indeed while he so traveled and rested, he did less and less in the literary line.

Although the reverent reception of the serialization of *Abraham Lincoln* fostered the publications of a collective volume of his *Poems* (1890). Yet, with the exception of a handful of poems published in periodicals, there would be no more literature from Hay's pen. That is not to say, however, that his fame as a writer diminished after 1890. It was sustained and, at times, enhanced by his active public life. Hay's politics, in the 1890s, were entirely national, and, in 1897, he secured the ambassadorial appointment to the Court of St. James's. In the course of his spectacularly successful tenure in England, his poems were rediscovered by the English and reprinted in London. Although he would claim that the call back to Washington marked an end to his long-desired peace and equanimity, he agreed to assume the position of secretary of state and arrived in the capital on the first of October 1898. Even had Hay wanted to resume his literary career (he wrote a poem now and then, including a sonnet to Theodore Roosevelt), he no longer had the time, energy, or spirit to do much.

Hay's literary fame began to wane, it seems, almost from the moment of his death. There were, in 1905, obligatory re-printings in journals of his poems, of the story "The Blood Seedling," and even though his authorship still had not been publicly acknowledged of *The Bread-Winners*. In 1906 his speeches and addresses were published, but collected therein were only the statements of an official known for his tact and his politics (not, it should be noted, the pieces he wrote in the 1870s for the *Tribune* on the Chicago fire or on the down-and-dirty politics of the 1880s). *Pike County Ballads*, this time with illustrations by N. C. Wyeth, was republished in 1912, and after it had become public knowledge that Hay was the author of *The Bread-Winners*, there appeared an edition in 1916, with an introduction by Clarence L. Hay, his son. These were followed, in 1916, by the publication of Hay's *Complete Poetical Works*. After 1916 very little of his work appeared in print, with the important exception of the appearance in 1939 of *Lincoln and the Civil War in the Diaries and Letters of John Hay*, a selection culled from the material of the 1860s left in manuscript for seven decades.

It may well be, as Howells concluded, that Hay, after the mid-1880s, decided not to turn again to literature, thereby renouncing what was still possible for him, to "be one of our first poets, one of our first novelists, one of our first essayists, as he certainly became one of our first historians."[7] But if there were lost opportunities, there were accomplishments: the Spanish essays, the realistically detailed short stories, the socio-economic novel with its brilliant portrait of the "self-made" girl and its hard-liner treatment of organized labor, the poems of narrative and statement, the biography of Lincoln, and the letters written by, in the words of Theodore Roosevelt, "The best letter-writer of his age."[8] Perhaps the way in which John Hay understood his successful life in letters and politics, best expressed in a "distich" he included in *Poems*, offers a way to measure it: "Try not to beat back the current, yet be not drowned in its waters; / Speak with the speech of the world, think with the thoughts of the few."[9]

Writing in 1916, Fred Lewis Pattee viewed John Hay's literary accomplishments in the brightest of lights. "Pike County Ballads" earned high marks, he thought. In that handful of poems Pattee saw evidence that Hay's "was one of those rare germinal minds that appear now and then to break into new regions and to scatter seed from which others are to reap the harvest." For the poems rang true at every point. "Their author had lived from his third until his thirteenth year in full view of the Mississippi River," wrote Pattee, "like Mark Twain he had played about the steamboat wharf, picking up the river slang and hearing the rude stories of the pilots and the deck hands. Warsaw, moreover, was on the trail of Western immigration, a place where all the border types might be studied." Hay also saw, later, "in Pittsfield, the countee seat of Pike County," the Pike "at home untouched by contact with others—the Golyers, the Frys, the Shelbys, and all the other drinkers of 'whisky-skins.'"[10]

The first three of the Pike County ballads—"Banty Tim," "Jim Bludso, of the Prairie Belle" and "Little Breeches"—catapulted Hay to immediate fame. Contemporary arguments over whether Hay or his friend Bret Harte had been the first to exploit the dialects of the American West served both to promote their fame and to delay the assessment of Hay's achievement. If there was no doubt that his poems captured the rhythmic speech of the Pike County man, the notion that such speech did not provide fit substance for poetry would long plague Hay. It was not immediately recognized that the poems were not primarily attacks on common poetic speech, but rather sly barbs aimed at the conventional morality of his day. In Jim Bludso he presents a hard-talking bigamist who is nevertheless capable of Christian self-sacrifice. This rude practitioner of a religion of humanity, according to the poet, could hardly suffer retribution from a true Christian God. If this poetically unconventional statement did not receive unanimous approval, it did tap a vein of it, largely unexpressed feelings. With tears in her eyes, it is said, George Eliot frequently recited by heart "Jim Bludso," and in *Ulysses* Joyce has Leopold Bloom on his way to the brothel, ruminate: "I did all a white man could . . . Jim Bludso. Hold her nozzle again the bank."

By 1923, Fred Lewis Pattee had shifted his attention from Hay's poems to his short stories. He regretted the fact that in the 1870s Hay's stories had been less influential in the development of the American short story than those of Bret Harte. "What might have been the result had John Hay and not Bret Harte been fated to direct the course of the short story through the 'seventies we may judge, perhaps, from his strong tale, 'The Blood Seedling,' . . . and that later story of his, 'A Foster Brother,' which so influenced Bronson Howard's drama 'Moorcroft.' As it is, two decades in the history of the short story form must be denominated the era of Bret Harteism—an era on the whole of small advance."[11]

One reason for Hay's failure to direct the course of the American short story through the 1870s was his own forfeiture of any such role, for "The Blood Seedling," published in 1871 when he was thirty-three, was to be his last completed story. While Bret Harte continued to write for magazines and to collect his stories into books that were immediately popular, Hay turned from the short story altogether, not even bothering at the last to collect the few stories he had written.

To talk about Hay's career as a short-story writer, then, is to deal with no more than a dozen years in a long, if sporadic, literary life. Even so, there is impressive range and significant variation in the stories we have. In them Hay experimented with several of the types of stories available to him. There are touches and hints of Washington Irving, Hawthorne, and his beloved Edgar Poe. But they remain only touches, after all, not borrowed patterns or imitated styles. It is clear from these stories that Hay was looking for his own style, his own fictional voice. It is also clear that in "The Blood Seedling" he found it, only to abandon promptly the short-story form altogether.

Even by way of introduction, there is much to say about Hay's stories; but we can limit ourselves to pointing to a few salient features. To suggest something of the evolution of Hay's themes and the development of his craft, it will be best to take up the stories in the probable order of their composition: "The Minstrel" (college work), "Red, White, and Blue," "Shelby Cabell," "The Foster-Brother," "Kane and Abel," "The Blood Seedling," and "The Life-Magnet."

John Hay's first known published fiction, nestled patriotically among line sketches of early Civil War scenes in *Harper's Weekly*, is perhaps the most calculated of his stories. Part of the reason for this is that the young author has a design upon his reader which involves something considerably different from the reader's entertainment or edification. "Red, White, and Blue" is a piece of fictionalized enlistment propaganda. Published early in the first year of the Civil War, the story is a morality piece defining for each young person in the North— male or female—the nature and extent of his Federal duty. Lincoln's young assistant was all-too-willing, apparently, to put in his own literary oar for the sacred cause of national unity. The story, then, tracing the impulses and vicissitudes of a romantic engagement threatened by the hero's three-month enlistment in the Union army concludes with the heroine's enlightened recognition that the union of personal, sexual love must be, in such days, subsumed, patriotically, to the love of Union. Living up to its title, the allegory very nearly defeats the tale. Not until the 1880s with the writing of *The Bread-Winners*, would Hay again so drastically, if far more skillfully, risk subordinating the needs of fiction to the dictates of propaganda.

"Shelby Cabell" (1866) is precisely the kind of story one would expect from the pen of a young American diplomat assigned to Paris. A piece of "international" fiction, it involves Americans ("Kentuckians"), footloose in Paris shortly after the Civil War, who become enmeshed in the love web woven by one Madame de

Bellechasse. But the love encounter is not between an American and a European, for, as was so often to happen in stories and novels by other American writers, the classically beautiful woman is a transplanted American, a Marquise who was born the daughter of "what the newspapers call a Merchant Prince." Of course she is a femme fatale who hopelessly enraptures Shelby Cabell. The author is himself too much of a romantic in this story to work out the profundities of the relationships he has set going, and the plot spins towards the melodramatic denouement of the hero's suicide. But the story, in several ways, is strangely predictive of Henry James's fiction of the next decade. Madame de Bellechasse, a young widow, anticipates James's eponymous heroine Madame de Mauves, who drives her husband, belatedly a devoted lover, to suicide, and his Christina Light, whose demands and denials cause the suicide of her American lover, Roderick Hudson. And the description of Madame de Bellechasse's father, a type close to Hay's heart, foreshadows James's portrayal of Christopher Newman in *The American* (1877). Here is Hay's version of an American "Merchant Prince":

> A man enriched by sagacious trade. If he had enlisted for a soldier, he would have been a General. If he had drifted into politics, a Senator. He was a square, grave, witty, shrewd, well-bred man, with a bald head and a white moustache, who could drive his own bargains and his own horses, and buy his own books and his own wine, and who wouldn't be condescended to by a prince, if a prince were ass enough to try it. A man whom no country on earth but America could send out. Everywhere

else it requires one life-time to make a fortune,
and three to learn how to spend it.

It is no wonder that when six years later the *Nation*
complained that Henry James's portrayal of Christopher
Newman was not "aesthetically attractive," John Hay was
moved to defend the appropriateness, the genuineness,
and the aesthetic worth of James's characterization.[12]
After all (though Hay did not say it), hadn't he himself in
Lorthrop Brinton, the father of Adele de Bellechasse,
sketched a worthy contemporary for Christopher
Newman?

For all its melodrama (the hero jumps to his death
from the Arche de Triomphe as his beloved drives by) and
its descriptive sensationalism ("I saw that my boots were
sprinkled with blood"), the story continues to interest the
reader. Hay was an original writer, if a minor artist.
Even his portrait of the disaffected Southerner after the
Civil War, stock-like and sketchy though the
achievement, anticipates Henry Adams's attempt in
Democracy (1880) and James's try in *The Bostonians*
(1885). Even Hay's use of the legend of Sam Patch, then
a fresh piece of folklore, as a way of introducing his own
hero's fascination with the idea of stylish suicide testifies
to the author's originality.

In a striking way, "The Foster-Brothers" (1869) is an
allegory on the themes of slavery, miscegenation, and
black versus white. The story is set in the Illinois towns
of "Thebes" and "Moscow" along the Mississippi. The
time of the story, though taking place "not many years
ago," is yet a time which has since seen "a continent . . .
dripped in blood" arise "from the red baptism cleansed of
its deadliest sin." This obvious reference to the Civil War
and to the peculiar institution of slavery comes in the
second paragraph of the story. At first it seems to be

merely the author's way of setting his tale in historical time. But in actuality this reference foreshadows the meaning of the story about to unfold.

The stranger who visits Moscow is a Southerner on a tour of the West and North, a journey taken at his father's behest. In antebellum days, the father has decided that the "north" will be "a foreign nation in a few years," and consequently he is anxious that his son "see something of the present regime." The plot depends much upon an initial coincidence: the visiting Southerner, Clarence Brydges, is taken with the charms and beauty of a midwestern belle, Miss Des Ponts. Mimi Des Ponts's father, a lawyer, is prosperous and highly-cultured. The author's description of the honorable Victor Des Ponts is deeply revealing:

> He was certainly a strikingly handsome man: a clear, dark skin; black eyes under straight brows; a square forehead and resolute jaw; the mouth almost concealed by a grizzled mustache, a feature not then so common as now; the whole face framed with glossy and luxuriant black curls. There was a strong general resemblance to his daughter; yet they were curiously unlike. The fine animal beauty of his face was in hers lit up and spiritualized by the glancing light of a vivid intelligence.

Consciously, the author intends his attitude to be favorable, but his racist assumptions bleed through the terms of his description. Victor Des Ponts's features—chin, jaw, eyes, "luxuriant" black curls—all add up to "fine animal beauty." The message is telegraphed and it is clear. We are in the presence of someone who is "passing" for white. Victor Des Ponts may be in every other way the white man's equal, but visually, and kinetically, he is different. We cannot help inferring that it is the salutary influence of his racist wife's white blood which has "spiritualized" his daughter's features.

Inevitably, love comes about between Victor Des Ponts's daughter and Clarence Brydges, and just as inevitably we move toward a confrontation between Victor Des Ponts and the elder Brydges. Less inevitably, that obligatory meeting occurs on the dark waters of the Mississippi (where Mark Twain would later place Huck and Jim on their odyssey away from political and social slavery), and it takes place when in the darkness of night Victor Des Ponts rescues a man who improbably turns out to be his "foster-brother" even as the river steamer that brought Brydges to Moscow burns in the distance. This archetypal confrontation between "foster-brothers," one black and a slave, the other white and that slave's master, turns on the intricacies of miscegenation. The white man's intransigent refusal to permit the marriage of his son to his former slave's daughter leads ineluctably to the river death of both fathers: "the foster-brothers went to the bottom locked in each other's arms." Ironically, their deaths are subsequently interpreted as the tragic result of an act of brotherly love, while the truth is that one death is a "fratricide" and the other a suicide.

The historical point of Hay's allegory is fairly clear. The blood bath that was the Civil War was necessary for the cleansing of the national soul. But the freedom of future generations might well demand the death of the un-reconstructed Southerner as well as that of the "passing" black man. For both, according to the terms of the allegory, are steeped in a common guilt. But the story does not stop here. When the slave carries his master down to death at the bottom of the river, Hay touches on an allegorical meaning that perhaps he himself did not want: blotting out the facts of heritage (through the death of the fathers) will enable the young couple to live out their lives, hostage only to that fortune which is uniquely theirs. Some critics will find flaws in "The Foster-Brothers" (its hopeful tone, for instance); others will find that, socially and historically, Hay's story has a lively and durable significance.

Published fifth and last, "Kane and Abel" (1871) may have been written before at least three of the other stories discussed here.[13] Like "Shelby Cabell," the story is set in Paris in the 1860s, and again it deals with the consequences of a fateful meeting between a young American male and a beautiful woman. Internal evidence tells us that the events of the story take place shortly before those of "Shelby Cabell." The stories share characters. Madame de Bellechasse, the femme fatale of "Shelby Cabell," plays a minor role in this story, as does Blair Harding (a slightly characterized version of the author). From "The Foster-Brothers" Hay borrows still another figure, Cade Marshall, who would also appear in "The Blood Seedling." But the principals, Kane and Abel Lennard, are unique to the story. They are twins from East Barrington, Massachusetts, newly arrived in Paris. Hay's first description of the twins is instructive:

They were precisely the same height, weight and build—slight, but superbly muscular—a very little taller than the average. As statues they would have been identical—form and features being exact copies of each other. But the coloring and the expression were totally different. Kane had a clear dark mat olive skin; hair black, crisply curling; black mustache, that made his even white teeth flash like lightning when he smiled. And he smiled perpetually.

Abel was blonde as a pure-blooded Visigoth in a straight line from Odin; gold hair, curled as if by the hot fingers of the sunshine; a mustache tinted like wheat, curving downward; and exquisite blue eyes, such as girls call poetical. He would have posed perfectly for an Adonaïs. But, in fact, he never wrote a rhyme in his life. Kane did, very neat verses.

On their conferred names, Hay writes: "'Why not?' he [the father] said to his wife. 'Your name is Kane and mine is Abel. Couldn't do better by searching a year.' Mrs. Lennard was blonde and her husband was dark; so she gave his name to the fair baby and hers to the dark one.'" Hay's decision to use the Cain-Abel archetype to organize his story of the fall of a New England latter-day puritan in sin-ridden Paris remains appropriate. Used directly, with only the simple reversal of roles—Abel, fulfilling his mother's binding wish that he will be his brother's keeper, kills Kane—the archetype serves to extend the suggestiveness of the story.

More interesting than his handling of the Romantic writer's favorite archetype, however, is Hay's decision to write another allegory. This time he centers on a young New Englander's fall from innocence in the ambience of Paris. Abel kills his brother to save him, and to protect the venerable Lennard family from the scandalous consequences of his marriage to a "sewing-girl" whose beauty does not quite cancel out either her passion for the cancan ("it is the quadrille gone mad, the quadrille wild, disheveled, frantic," cries the author-narrator) or her shadowy alliance to a grotesque, almost subhuman, Jew. The madness within the fears which arise from such social mismatching is made apparent in an exchange between Madame de Bellechasse and her father (the self-made Merchant Prince, as he is called in "Shelby Cabell"):

"*Quelle horreur!*" cried Adele. "Alice writes
that Tom Webster has married his cook."

"Disgusting enough!" said Mr. Brinton. "I
had heard of it."

"And then she adds, that she is a very good
sort of woman—as if that was any excuse."

"No excuse perhaps, but at least some alleviation. Vulgarity may be reformed in the course of years. I think the only impossible marriage is one with vulgarity and vice. Death is a bad thing—but death is preferable to that!" Spoken in the presence of Abel Lennard, who has that moment received the news that his brother is about to make an even more disreputable marriage, these words establish the social norm of the New England Lennards—as well as, it might be added, approximating the author's. Personally, Hay was disturbed over the way American "innocents" behaved in Europe; everywhere, in ignorance, they ran the greatest social risks."[14] Henry James was to make this observation into one of his principal themes. Hay possessed neither James's persistent talent nor his genius, but in "Kane and Abel," as in "Shelby Cabell," he tried his hand, years before James, at what was to be a sustained allegory of American innocence on trial before the social courts of Europe.

"The Blood Seedling" (1871) is something more than John Hay's finest story.[15] It is fiction of some distinction, especially remarkable given its date of composition and publication. Re-reading it, one again laments, with Pattee, that this story had so little effect upon the course of the American short story.

Introducing the Warsaw family life he would draw upon in the Pike County ballads (Colonel Blood, for instance, and the Golyers), Hay abandoned both the theme of American innocence defeated by European experience and the theme of racial fear and miscegenation, to pursue the equally promising, and personally more congenial, theme of rural tragedy among simple farm people. "The Blood Seedling" presents a situation which recalls the interest of Nathaniel Hawthorne. The idea of guilt which lies fallow and unexpiated for twenty years is reminiscent, particularly, of "Roger Malvin's Burial" and *The Scarlet Letter*; while the evening visit of Hay's prosperous farmer to a crazed medium shows the traces, possibly, of Goodman Brown's presence at the Black Man's unholy rites. But it is not this affinity with Hawthorne's fiction which accounts for the overall power of Hay's story. To get at that, one must look to style, authorial tone, the tale's firm construction, and, more specifically, Hay's sure handling of the tale's central symbol, the apple seedling ("Blood's Seedling grape") prophetically named for Colonel Blood.[16]

There can be no doubt that Hay wrote this story out of root experience. He decided to write about those individuals who are sometimes dismissed genially if facilely as "good country people." He would show that within such individuals existed a potential for malevolence and evil, along with an equal capacity for virtue: which was to remind us that there existed as well a full potential for tragedy. Out of that "colorless and commonplace picture of rural Western life" (Hay's words), there emerged a forceful story of the destiny that a man's own heart can make for him.

Secretly committing murder at the very time that he plants the apple seedling which will symbolize his portion of a happy and prosperous life, Allen Golyer sows the seed for his own knowledge of evil. Having killed out of love and anger, the young farmer regains his childhood sweetheart, marries her, and prospers for twenty years. In no apparent way does his secret crime affect his outward life. But the knowledge of evil will out, it seems, and the author, in a decidedly strong stroke, structures Golyer's moral retribution in a credibly "Western" way. Through an indifferent, distracted, neurasthenic medium whose emotional life was been nurtured on that cynosure of the nineteenth century, Emanuel Swedenborg, the unfortunate farmer has revealed to him at last what, in his compulsion, he would fear: the details of his ancient crime and the publication of the fact that his guilt remains unexpiated.

There are other fine touches in the story. For example, Bertie Leon, the bagman for the St. Louis house of Draper & Mercer who becomes Golyer's victim, is typically dandified, philandering, and urbanely corrupt, penetrating the more innocent hamlets of the "West" to seduce their prime maidens. But for all his guile and his corruption, he does not manage to commit murder. That sin is reserved for the seemingly uncomplicated farmer, whose open ways and rude manner are no match for the articulate drummer. A second example. Employing "the Blood seedling" to open and to close the Golyer tragedy, and as a recurrent motif as well, the author allows the meaning of that symbol to emerge gracefully and powerfully. With deftness he turns the seedling into a symbol for prosperity and goodness, laid out for his characters, before he allows the same seedling to swell into the reader's symbol for evil. The narrative, from start to finish, is told with authorial sureness and in the even-tempered tone we expect of a particular kind of artist at his maturity. The author reveals his principals as he has come to know them, with no highlights or special effects forced at their expense. In the decade marked by Bret Harte's sentimentalism, and a full two decades before Hamlin Garland offered his bleakly realistic stories of the agrarian "west," John Hay wrote a strong tale that unfolds its universal meaning with the very rhythm and pace of human experience.

In "The Blood Seedling" John Hay moved away from his earlier themes, discovering, at one fell swoop it would seem, his most effective fictional voice. It is lamentable that he chose not to work his claim. It is also understandable, given the circumstances of Hay's life in 1870-71, that, after a daily stint as editorial writer for the *Tribune*, he would have, evenings and Sundays, neither the time nor the energy to write full-blown short stories. Yet Pike County, still present in memory and imagination, found its creative outlet in the ballads that, inspired by the slightly earlier performances of Bret Harte (especially "Chiquita," "Dow's Flat" and "Plain Language from Truthful James"), flowered in the pages of the *New York Tribune* in late 1870 and 1871.

Into those ballads went the materials and energies that would, in an earlier, less all-consuming time, have gone into the more leisurely elaborated short stories he was wont to write in the 1860s.

Not for a dozen years after he joined the staff of the *Tribune* would Hay return to fiction, and by the time he did so he had himself cornered a few choice lots and had become more interested in the propagandistic potential of the popular novel than in its potential for portraying the varieties of life and laying bare the verities of character. In a sense, the novel he wrote in 1883, *The Bread-Winners*, constituted still another departure for Hay, for its writing was an act altogether typical, after all, of the author's entire life. Hay would not rest in one place, with one form or theme, long enough to consolidate gains. No sooner did the writer complete a first experiment than he skipped on to something else. It is somehow characteristic that in the twenty-one years remaining to him after *The Bread-Winners*, Hay would write no second novel, despite the fact that his first attempt at novel-writing had been both a commercial and a critical success. Poetry he would continue to write to the end of his life, of course, even during his seven years as America's first modern secretary of state, but by 1883 John Hay had finished with prose fiction. All that was left to him by way of extended writing was the monumental *Abraham Lincoln: A History*. Before him, of course, still lay that long stretch of national service at the turn of the century, a period in which his fame at times rivaled that of Theodore Roosevelt himself.

NOTES

[1] *The Education of Henry Adams* (Boston and New York: Houghton Mifflin, 1918), p. 503.

[2] "John Hay in Literature," *North American Review* (Sept. 1905), 181: 343.

[3] *A Poet in Exile: Early Letters of John Hay*, ed. Caroline Ticknor (Boston and New York: Houghton Mifflin, 1910), pp. 18-19.

[4] MS letter, David Gray to John Hay, Dec. 24, 1872, John Hay Papers, John Hay Library, Brown University, Providence, R. I. Quoted with consent.

[5] See George Monteiro, "John Hay and the Union Generals," *Journal of the Illinois State Historical Society* (Feb. 1976), 69: 46-66, and *Henry James and John Hay: The Record of a Friendship* (Providence, R.I.: Brown University Press, 1965), pp. 62-65.

[6] William Roscoe Thayer, *The Life and Letters of John Hay* (Boston and New York: Houghton Mifflin, 1915), 1: 386.

[7] Howells, "John Hay in Literature," 350.

[8] *The Letters of Theodore Roosevelt*, ed. Elting E. Morison et al. (Cambridge, Mass.: Harvard University Press, 1951-54), 6: 1490.

[9] *The Complete Poetical Works of John Hay*, intr. Clarence L. Hay (Boston and New York: Houghton Mifflin, 1916), p. 185.

[10] *A History of American Literature Since 1870* (New York: Century, 1916), p. 91.

[11] *The Development of the American Short Story: An Historical Survey* (New York: Harper, 1923), pp. 286-87.

[12] *Nation* (Jan. 11, 1877), 29; Thayer, *Life of John Hay*, 1: 394-95. It is interesting to record Hay's claim that "Shelby Cabell" was actually a "description" of a man and a woman he had met in Paris. The sketch is "not very good," he admitted, but it is "very true," adding that in such cases, "one must make a choice: between esthetic effect and realism" (Hay to Young, Oct. 9, 1866, and Hay to [Harriet?] Loring, July 18, 1866—"Press Copy Letters from the Legations in Paris and Vienna, July 1865—Sept. 1867," John Hay Papers. Quoted with consent.

[13] "Kane and Abel" was not published until Apr. 1871, though it had been sold to Frank Leslie by May, 1869. See MS letter, Hay to Nicolay, May 14, 1869, John Hay Papers.

[14] See, for example, Hay's anonymous remarks on James's heroine Daisy Miller in "Girlhood on the American Plan," *Atlantic Monthly* (Mar., 1879), 43: 399-401; reprinted in Monteiro, *Henry James and John Hay*, 62-65.

[15] Both the New York *Times* and the *New York Tribune* praised the story. On Feb. 21, 1871, the *Tribune* called it "a weird and powerful story which will attract attention as a fresh growth in the sterile waste of magazine fiction, coloring a tragic narrative with vivid pictures of Western life and character" (p. 6). Two days later, the *Times* called it both "original" and "strong." "We hope the

author will write more short stories," it continues; "this is the field of our current literature which somehow bears the fewest flowers, and which it would be the most profitable to cultivate" (p. 2). In the same month, reviewing *Castilian Days*, the *Galaxy* noted that John Hay was now simply "the most promising of young American Prose writers" (Dec. 1871, 12: 867).

[16] There did exist a grape called the "Blood Seedling"; see "The Grapes," *The Cultivator* (Feb. 1862), 10: 58.

THE STORIES

Shelby Cabell (1866)

My acquaintance with Shelby Cabell began in a queer sort
of way. I was crossing the Pont Neuf late one night,
returning from an evening spent with some friends in the
Rue Tournon to my lodgings in the Champs Elysées. It
was not the nearest way home. I could have made better
time by going along the quai to the Pont de la Concorde.
But I always liked to loaf through Old Paris—*le Paris qui
s'en va*—when I could; and there are few spots more
engaging to a man with a taste for the mouldy than those
fine relics of the times of the Fourth Henry, the Rue
Dauphine, and Place Dauphine, and the quiet quarters
that form at either end of the bridge a sort of *tête-de-pont*
to resist the encroachments of demolition and change. So
I used to go a little out of my way, returning from the
Latin Country to the fresh drab avenues of the Elysian
Fields, to pass through those fine old haunts of the fast
people of two centuries gone, and have my little protest
against the barbarisms of civilization. The night I speak
of I was going over my customary plaint: "Ill fares the
nation where the present snubs the past—the poets have
no show in this age— picturesqueness and dirt have lost
their charm—the municipal council will soon begin to
make knife-handles of the bones of the dead"; but it was
late, and I had passed the evening in good company.
Near the middle of the bridge I perceived a man standing
motionless in the road. As I came nearer he started, ran,
and leaped upon the high stone balustrade overlooking
the river. His hat fell off as he jumped, and as he
balanced himself on his perch with outstretched arms his
long light hair streamed out in the wind, and gave him an
odd, uncanny look. I sprang toward him, caught him by

the clothes, and dragged him down from his dangerous pedestal. In my excitement, forgetting I was in France, I said, "What are you about?" As he gazed at me coolly an instant without answering, I said, "*Pardon, Monsieur, mais que faites vous là?*"

He picked up his hat, and brushing it with his sleeve, said, "I like your first phrase best. I speak English full as well as French, and I reckon you do too."

"Yes, but what business has a Kentuckian taking a plunge-bath in the Seine at midnight?"

He looked sharply at me. "How do you know I am a Kentuckian?"

"I *reckoned so*," I answered. He laughed and shook hands.

"A fair shot," he said. "We fellows from the woods have always some loose joint in our armor. Where do you hail from?"

"Nor far from you, I should think: Fayette County."

"Hurrah for the Blue Grass!" he shouted. "This is a godsend. You are the first neighbor I have met in an age. Let's go and take a drink."

"Of course," I replied. "But you don't seem to me like a man who was on the point of drowning himself five minutes ago."

"Oh no! I had no idea of doing it to-night. I just got up on the wall there to see how it would look, if a man were ready to try it. And, by-the-way, talking about drowning yourself, I have an old grudge against that useless point of land down there, the Vert-Galant. It would be a very neat thing to go off the shoulders of the Béarnais with a plunge and a splash, if one could light in deep water; but those green trees and the moist turf below would let you down with a few bruises. If you could get on the neck of the bronze horse, with plenty of spring in your legs and arms, you could do it leap-frog fashion, over the head of the King. It would be quite sensational on a bright afternoon when the bridge is full of passengers!"

He walked up as he talked to the equestrian statue of Henry IV, which stands in its spacious alcove, midway of the bridge, staring, horse and rider, into the narrow opening of the Place Dauphine, waiting and watching for something that never issues from the damp and quiet court. The moonlight touching to a softer expression the wide eyes and the firm mouth of the great Bourbon, one could fancy that his image smiled at the grotesque fancy of the strange creature at my side.

"But it's no use talking about that," he said, turning away. "Until they clear away that snout of the island the jump would be only ridiculous."

"Especially," I replied, "for a countryman of Sam Patch."

We were walking through the dark little Rue de la Monnaie, toward the Rue de Rivoli. My companion lifted his hat respectfully.

"You have just pronounced, he said, "the greatest name of our times. I hope you share my admiration for Patch!"

"Hardly, I am afraid. In fact I know nothing of him, except that he began as a loafer, flourished by bravado, and died from an awkward jump when tipsy."

"A base calumny, Sir, born of envy, and kept alive by the tendency of men to deride the great deeds they dare not emulate and can not understand." This was said with great earnestness, though quietly enough. "I know all about him. A year ago I thought as you do, and I hope to be forgiven for my foolish sneers because of the sincerity of my repentance. I have carefully studied his life and character, and I am sure that all these incidents of his career that astonished the world were simply experiments as to the *best way of doing it*. Profoundly disgusted with life he passed his last days in searching boldly and laboriously the best way of quitting it. There is a deep philosophy in all this. I believe that the style in which a man enters the next world depends on the manner in which he quits this. Pshaw! It is too simple for argument. Did not Caesar fold his robes as he fell? Does not Miss M'Flimsey put on her drawing-room air before she passes the threshold of the antechamber?"

"This chap is clearly mad," I said to myself, "but the method is a little new to me."

"Follow Patch," he continued, as we turned into the Rue de Rivoli, and walked along the brilliant street toward the Louvre—"follow him from the first plunge he made from the roof of a five-story factory, in Pawtucket, into the Blackstone River, then from High Bridge, until at last the terror and beauty of Niagara lured him, and he came to be a nine days' wonder for the tourist, to whom he was no more than a hero is to his valet. A smaller mind would have said, 'Here is the place for the end.' But Patch, with the instinct of genius, saw that Niagara was too great for him. Nature crushes all human effect there. The frame was too big for the picture. And it was this consideration that made him spread his umbrella for a parachute, in those Titanic leaps that show what a craven Death is, when you know how to take him. When he was ready—I know he *was* ready, for when they fished him out three days afterward they found only a bad quarter in his pocket—he went to Genesee Falls, and there, in the midst of that quiet and beautiful nature that harmonized so well with an act of moral grandeur like his, he plunged and went through to his own place. He is the Ideal

Suicide."

"You evidently have very little respect," I said, "for the 'canon 'gainst self-slaughter.'"

"Don't mistake me. Suicide in general is not a good thing. It is only a thing to do in exceptional circumstances. But when done it should be well done. This is the glory of Patch—that having resolved to die, he sought through months of travel and experiment the best way of dying. The world has never caught the true meaning of his strange device: 'Some things can be done AS WELL as others.' Blind eye, that can not read in the light of his death the word of the sublime enigma!"

We turned up the Rue Castiglione, and cast our eyes—as does every one emerging from the long colonnade to cross the Rue St. Honoré, up to the colossal figure of the First Consul, gazing southward through the mists of midnight, as if the bronze eyes were fixed on Corsica.

"A man ought to go out with a flash, like stars, candles, rockets, and most bright things," continued my companion. "That Emperor up there, for instance. If he could not have had the luck of a bullet at Waterloo, why hadn't he the wit, after talking things over with Montalivat, at the Hôtel Lambert, and confessing that all was lost—to come up here, mount that column, and use his *droit au vol*? The finest opportunity for an effect that ever was thrown away! Imagine the superb chance he had: to come out on the summit of that monument of his own glory, and stand in his own true garb, gray over-coat and cocked hat, beside that classic ideal: look his last on the Tuileries and the Invalides and go to heaven—by way of the pavement. The adoring world would have gathered up the scattered relics of the real man, while the Ideal Image would still have stood on high, defying the storms of heaven and history."

We had crossed the Place and entered the Rue de la Paix. He turned and said, "I wonder no one thought of that at the Hôtel Lambert that night. But I suppose he would no more have listened to it then than he does now. *Ohé Lambert!*" he cried. But the outraged statue kept his bronze eyes fixed on Corsica.

Walking toward the Boulevard, he said, "In general there are objections to going off that column. It would not be neat to light on the railings at the bottom, and besides, you might kill an Invalide of the Guard."

We sat down to our coffee at the Café Napolitain.

I began with the sacramental question of school-boys; "What's your name?"

He said, "Guess it. You guessed my State."

"Merriwether, Cabell, Marshall, Shelby—"

"There, that will do. Shelby Cabell is enough. I'll try yours. Woolfolk, Peyton, Clay, Rowan, Blair—"

"And Harding." I supplied the patronymic.

"I swear," said Cabell, "I can smell the Blue Grass when I hear such names."

We talked of home. If Cabell was mad, as I had begun to suspect, the evil spirit vanished at the awaking of old memories. We rained questions upon each other. Where did you go to school? What has become of Joe Coleman? Whom do you know in Lexington? What sort of fellow did Miss Peyton marry? Any relation to the Logans of Loganport? We talked of old scenes and old friends, until we forgot the Boulevard and its flashing lights and roaring wheels; the savage freshness of the hills, the vast solitudes of the prairies came back to me. I heard around me the slow pouring of water from carafes to absinthe goblets, but I only thought how, under the early starlight, the water was dancing down the white ravine, past an old plantation on Green River. I heard the clatter of tumblers and spoons, and thought of the tinkling of cow-bells in the dim woods and willowy waterside of the Great West.

We sat there until the "little ladies" had spread their trailing plumes and rustled away, and the Cocodès had bored each other to the desired somnolence, and the lights were dead, the bummers fled, and all but us departed. A heavy-eyed Ganymede approaches.

"*Pardon, Messieurs, mais*"—and his shoulders go up to his ears.

"True, it *is* late: *l'addition.*"

"Where do you live?" (Together.)

"Champs Elysées 61."

"Rue Racine 2."

"Come and see me."

"Of course. I don't find a Fayette County man lying around loose often enough not to appreciate one when I stumble over him."

From that time forward I saw a great deal of Shelby Cabell. At first I thought him a little deranged, but after I knew him better I considered his frequent references to suicide in its aesthetic phases a harmless affectation, which though sometimes tiresome was oftener amusing. If from time to time a vague suspicion came to me that there was a deeper and more painful interest in this subject to Cabell than appeared, it vanished when I met him again. For he was almost always gay, hearty, and all alive. He intensely enjoyed seeing his own theories burlesqued, and took a keen relish in running into absurdity his own ghastly fancies. He always announced his intention of "going off that way sometime," but always lightly, even jestingly. It was at first unpleasant to hear so grim a subject so frequently mentioned even in jest, but I at last grew accustomed to it, and even amused at the infinite variety of his gory reveries. The Western people are all more or less original and individual, and their characters are as hard to polish as diamonds. They carry their knobbiness and their sharp angles through all the friction of time and society. They are hard to polish, but they are as hard to corrupt. Vice breaks her teeth on them. Even the frightful solvent of slavery has not been enough to melt down the rugged virtues of the Kentucky character. It has left stains, of course, but they do not go below the surface. Shelby Cabell was a fair type of these people.

He was of good height, spare build, not perfectly erect. The Kentuckian grows fast, and when young has a slight stoop in the shoulders, which disappears with the slenderness of youth. At fifty he is portly and straight as an arrow. He had very good eyes; that is, they were well set, wide apart, brows gracefully arched; the eyes themselves were like all gray eyes. The expression of his face in repose was grave. His complexion was dark, too dark to suit perfectly the hair and eyes; but that you see continually among the people in the Mississippi Valley. There is a certain richness of organization that embrowns, under a Western sun, a face that would have been blonde any where else. Men blush brown out West, never pink. He was put together rather loosely, but a man would have made an unlucky mistake in selecting him for an adversary. In a row he would be as sure, and as quick, and as merciless as a piece of steel machinery.

He was generally well dressed, though a little carelessly. He was not scrupulous in his cravats. His hats were too apt to suggest the *Ecole de Medecine*. But his crowning offense was his hair. The golden fleece which he brandished in the face of society was just cause for social ostracism. I appealed to him to sacrifice that much to the Decencies.

"Sorry I can't oblige you," he said, laughingly, "but I think long yellow hair is a fine feature in the picture of a fellow 'going off' from a given point. It gives him the effect of a comet. I got the idea from a painting of a lost lady plunging from London Bridge."

He had been abroad about four years. His father had died the year before he sailed, leaving his fortune to be divided in three portions among his sons. Shelby, the second son, took all of his patrimony in money and funds. The elder took the home plantation, and the cadet the estate coming from the mother, who died when they were children, on the Tennessee border. When the rebellion broke out, the older brother went into the National Army, the younger joined the revolt, and Shelby, stuffing his worldly gear into a carpet-bag, went to Richmond to seek service in the Regular Army of the Confederate States. There he met the Honorable Epaminondas Strutt, who was about sailing for Europe in a diplomatic capacity. The Honorable and high-toned Epaminondas wanted a Secretary of Legation, as he had heard it was the thing for diplomats to be accompanied by an appendage so styled, though his ideas of what were the duties incident to that function were of the vaguest. But young Cabell, who was burning with ardor for what was called "ouah cause," and whose young imagination was also perhaps a little touched by indiscreet reading, was delighted with this opportunity of serving his embryo nation in the gay capitals of Europe. It was a sweet thing, doubtless, to die for one's country, but not a bitter one to live for it in the town where the Chevalier de Faublas had flourished, and the Lady of the Camelias had queened it, for her hour. So he was proud and happy, when, one night in the bar-room of the Spotswood House, the unctuous and effusive statesman grasped his hand, and said: "My gifted young friend, your father was my most intimate and trusted comrade on many a well-fought field—political, I would say. We fought the hellhounds of abolition together here. I have selected your father's son out of sixteen applicants, to continue that fight on a furrin shore. No thanks, Sir," waving a pudgy hand with a splendid magnanimity and moving to the door.

Cabell stood a moment with his head in the clouds, until the bar-tender said, "Is you or the Judge gwine to pay for them drinks?"

"Oh, I! How much?"

"Eleven juleps; two brandy straight; a lemon he put in his pocket; and a tumbler he throwed at a dorg—two dollars and eighty-five cents—say three dollars for luck."

Cabell's duties as Secretary of Legation, thus begun, continued in much the same way. They came to a sudden and brilliant close after a few months' residence in Paris. One evening at his rooms in the Grand Hotel, Shelby saw his high-toned and chivalrous chief grossly, awkwardly, yet successfully, cheating at Bluff. He went to the table, seized the arm of the high-toned, etc., took an ace from his cuff and drew it across his cheek. He then took the sugar-tongs from the side-board and with them seized firmly the blooming nose of the high-toned, and led him to the door. He came back, and threw the sugar-tongs out of the window. "Gentlemen," he said, "will you drink to my retreat from the Diplomatic service of our country?"

In the morning he received a letter dismissing him from "the service." The Honorable Epaminondas wrote that he had been informed by a high-toned and reliable gentleman that Cabell had been educated at a New

England College, and had there doubtless imbibed radical and disorganizing notions, which rendered him incapable of holding an office of such delicacy and trust as Secretary to a Confederate States Plenipotentiary. He said he would report his action in the case to the President, who would doubtless be grieved, as he was, at the unworthiness of one he had loved and trusted. Not one word of the scene of the night before.

Shelby's illusions died hard, but they perished one by one. Thus deprived of all opportunity of serving the cause he worshiped—for the letter of Strutt would, of course, be conclusive against him at Richmond—he grew restless and discontented. He gradually broke with most of the refugees in Paris. He soon discovered that his apparent popularity was only due to his lavish extravagance, and his presumed wealth. His first efforts at retrenchment convinced him of that. He had been young and credulous enough to dream that he was loved for himself. When he first talked one evening about a simple pastoral ménage in the country, he was answered by pretty badinage and caresses that made him forget his theme. The second time a pair of plump shoulders were shrugged petulantly, and the red lips said with some energy, "*Mais, c'est une scie.*" He determined one day to come to an understanding. His fair enslaver lived in the Avenue Marigny. As he reached the corner of the Faubourg St. Honoré he saw her alighting from her carriage. She was with the Comte de Playoff, a young Russian who had just come down to Paris to beggar his heart and get rid of a few millions. He followed them up to her apartment. His ring was not answered for some minutes. When the saucy face of the *bonne* appeared he started to enter. She stood in the way, and said, "*Madame n'y est pas.*"

"You lie!" said the furious boy; but suddenly struck with a desire to be further assured, he said, kindly, "Pardon me, Lisette, but I am sure she has entered. Ask again, and say it is I."

The girl went through the ante-chamber and into the salon. In a moment she reappeared and said, "Madame is going to the country tomorrow, and is desolate not to see Monsieur; but it is impossible: she is too busy. She will be happy to meet Monsieur next winter if Monsieur finds himself in Paris."

She shut the door in his face. The Kentuckian drew back his fist to smash the panel, but thought better of it and went home, deeply disgusted and humiliated. He was not jealous, because his time had not come to love.

These incidents, and many others he recounted to me from time to time, rubbed the butterfly-dust very rapidly from the wings of his illusions. He was getting blasé almost before he was grown. His restlessness became invincible. He wandered over Europe and into Asia for two years. He squandered most of his property. He exhausted most of the amusements which young men work so conscientiously to exhaust. He did the regular things that every body must do who aspires to sit in the august congregation of the Fast.

He had now come back to Paris to "spend the evening of his days," he said, "tranquilly. The pomps and glories of the world charm me no more. I taste the joys reserved for the philosopher. I wear a bad hat. I shove no pasteboard. I wear no gloves. I read some books. I see some plays, as thou dost, Antony. I have no wife, no child, no country. I have no heroes to worship. My President was caught the other day scudding through a corn-field in his wife's shawl and gyasticutum, I believe they call it. All my old masters in the theory and practice of secession have taken the iron-clad oath. I don't want to be reconstructed. I have been a secessionist ever since I was born, and I can't lie about it. The cause is gone in disaster and disgrace, but I don't think it will pay to take the victor's oath for the few days I have to live."

One day I said to him, "Providence is clearly against suicide at present. An officer of the Lanciers in the Rue de la Ville-l'Evêque made up his mind to quit this world yesterday. He fell on his sword. It pierced him from point to hilt, but dodged every vital spot. Without waiting to draw it out he seized his razor and made two savage cuts at his throat. His razor scorned to touch his windpipe or jugular. Disgusted, he cocked his Derringer and fired into his left temple. The flash burned his hair and scorched his eyelashes, but the ball skimmed round between skin and skull and got out on the other side. He staggered to his bed, but in a moment discovered he was not yet in heaven, and rushed to his window (he lived *au cinquième*) and vaulted over his balcony—"

"Sensible at least," said Cabell; "he should have commenced with that!"

"But at that instant an upholsterer's wagon filled with feather-beds passed, and received him fainting. The boy who drove was frightened out of a year's growth at this addition to his load—a mad Frenchman, with a staff sword spitting him through the body, a Derringer still grasped in his fist, and a gaping bullet hole on each side of his head. They took him to a hospital, and to-day Dr. Peloton, from whom I have the story, tells me he will be ready for duty in a fortnight."

"Poor fellow!" said Shelby, with real sympathy; "he will be so demoralized by a failure like that that he will never try it again. A man can't be too careful and cool in such matters. I saw a superb piece of work not long ago.

A young fellow in my street had gotten tired of this make-shift world, and especially of this Old-Clo' Empire. He knew a little English also, and read Carlyle. He had become imbued with the great Scotchman's philosophy—'this world is for the strong and the mighty; if you are not strong and mighty shut your mouth, and don't maunder about those who are; if that is hard, you can die—that's always easy'; and he concluded to die. He bought an ordinary axe, and after taking out the helve, he fastened a pair of dumb-bells to the ends of the blade. He drove a staple tightly into his ceiling. He tied a cord to his axe and passed it through the staple. With the cord in his hand he lay down on the floor, placing his head in a circle he had drawn on the planks with chalk. Raising his axe to the ceiling by means of this simple machinery, he adjusted his head so that the fine blue edge of the steel was precisely over his eyes—and let go. I went into the room two days after. His concierge had come to me, not knowing where he could be, and having seen us sometimes together; and I went to the Inspector of my quarter. We went up together. It was a dead shot. Struck fair in the eyes and chipped off the top of the head, as you split an apple."

"Confound you, Cabell!" I protested—"this specialty of yours grows sometimes too horrible to be amusing."

"Not amusing, perhaps," he said, "but rather edifying. Yet it is sad to think that the great geniuses who do a good thing in this way can tell us nothing about it. All we really know is derived from the frivolous bunglers who balk at the gates. There is one thought that as often as it occurs to me strikes me with horror."

His brow contracted as he spoke, and he clenched his hands and teeth like a strong man in bodily pain. After a moment he continued:

"You know you think very fast in rapid motion. A swift sailing boat in a gale—a fast horse flying against the wind—wake up your mind to an amazing activity. I have never thought so fast and so freely as when I used to steal my father's blood-horses out of the stable and ride quarter-races in the moonlight with the Merriwether boys. I can't help fearing—and shuddering at it—that when a man finds his life so snarled and twisted that he must drop it as a bad job, and so goes off from some given point"—this was Cabell's favorite expression: amidst all his eccentricities he was always faithful to his preference of a great leap and plunge as the proper way to quit this world—"he may find in the busy second of his fall, that what seemed so impossible was the simplest thing in the world; and he may see the very means of gaining his life's set prize, so dearly longed for and miserably despaired of, blazing before his sickening brain. The very air as it whistles by him may hiss in his ringing ears *how it might have been done*! I tell you, Harding, that gravels *me* sometimes!"

"And I tell you, Cabell, that is the first sensible word I have heard you utter on this subject. I can't conceive a more pitiable figure than that of a suicide in the next world. It will be like that we sometimes cut in troubled dreams, when we find ourselves in a bright salon crowded with very fine company, and suddenly perceive we have omitted to put on our trowsers."

Cabell would rarely discuss the abstract question of suicide. He pretended to consider that a settled matter for himself. But he was always ready to treat of the comparative advantages of different styles of self-destruction. He contended sturdily for the attraction of gravitation as the best and most artistic agent for the purpose. That given, he was not bigoted as to place and time. He had the heights of the principal monuments of Paris noted down in his tablets, with a careful computation of the progressive velocity of a body falling from pinnacle to pavement. He seemed to delight in the bristling array of figures which expressed the frightful momentum of a weight of 149 pounds (he weighed that in his boots) increasing as the square of the distance traversed.

"Nôtre Dame," he said, "would be a superb point of departure. A clean, sheer fall from the front façade on the pave. But Heaven only knows when the demolitions will be over, and you don't want to come down on a heap of rubbish and mason's tools. And, really, one does not feel entirely comfortable in following in the wake of Claude Frollo.

"The Tour St. Jacques la Boucherie is more finished and compact. It is especially convenient, since they have covered the saint's back with gas-fixtures for illuminations, by which you can climb to his hat, and bid good-by to the Old Paris, with nothing between you and heaven. But if one is going to do the ecclesiastical thing at all, he might as well buy a third-class ticket to Strasbourg, and take his flight from the greatest spire in the world."

He generally concluded by saying, "After all, the Arc de l'Etoile is good enough for the likes o' me."

The better I knew Cabell the more I wondered at his odd affectation, for I thought it nothing else. He was so cool and imperturbable, and so genial and cordial; his views of life were, with this exception, so just, and his health, above all, so perfect, that I never dreamed he was in earnest. At the same time this fanciful style of speech was utterly out of character. He was not a man you would expect to hear babbling for the mere sake of babble.

Therefore, though never really disquieted, I was often puzzled by his talk. I had as yet seen no adequate cause for the entire indifference to life he professed. When you see a man hopelessly crushed and ruined, bankrupt of life and hope, you ask, "Who was she?" I could not see, in the greatest freedom of Cabell's confidences, any sign that a single one of the many tenants that had flitted in and out of his heart had ever, like Claude Duval, carved her name on its walls.

The Western man has a great gift of silence in these matters. Yet he never seems to expect it in others. I should not have thought of confiding a serious love-affair to Cabell. But as he never mentioned any thing of the kind to me I concluded there was nothing worth mentioning. Illogical, but natural enough.

One afternoon he and I were at my windows in the Champs Elysées. The avenue was filled with its usual chaos of carriages rolling to the Bois de Boulogne. Shelby was in his pleasantest vein. His satire was always sunny and fresh; never morbid and poisonous as a man's wit is apt to grow in Paris. He sat in the warm golden light, twisting his yellow mustache, and talking in his quaint, half-sleepy way about a project he had once cherished of constructing a Bois de la Fayette near the race-track at Lexington, describing, with a quiet verve that was inimitable, the teams and the toilets that the beauty and fashion of the Blue Grass Region would have displayed there. I heard hard swearing below my windows and looked out. A *voiture de place* lumbering down the hill, had struck the wheel of another laboring up, and there was a crash, and a jam, and a temporary halt of the long line of vehicles. I saw the blood bays of the exquisite Marquise de Bellechasse reined back on their haunches, and behind them a Daumont, full of the prettiest toilet and the prettiest woman in Paris. She gave me a languid nod of recognition, as the postillions saw a break in the line and dashed by.

Cabell gazed at the equipage like a man mesmerized, his hands clenched, a bright spot burning on his cheek, his lips half open, his whole life blazing in his fixed gray eyes. I looked at him with astonishment. His face was new and strange to me.

In a moment he sank back in his chair and fell to twisting his mustache again.

"Well, what did you see?" I asked.

"The door of my closet flew open and I saw my skeleton," he answered, as if at random, like a sleepy child.

"What, Madame de Bellechasse?" I cried.

"Yes," he said, in his usual tone, "though it does require some clairvoyance to see a skeleton under those beautiful lines, and Madame 'would not like to consider herself, nor yet to be so considered, in that bony light'"— quoting Dickens, as many of us do, when we want to close an embarrassing inquisition or argument. Mr. Boffin, and Captain Cuttle, and Richard Swiveller have helped me out of more tight places than all my friends together.

That evening Cabell, as he was going, said, "Lend me a hundred or two francs."

I gave him the bills.

"Shall I write you a note?"

I had never taken a promissory note before from a friend. But a new idea had come to me. I imagined a use for one. So I said "Yes, there are pens and paper. Write it in French."

He looked up inquiringly, but as I made no further explanation, he wrote the note, which I laid away.

The next day I dined with an old Washington friend,

whom I had known as an attaché of the French Legation. Two titles and as many fortunes had fallen upon him through the timely kindness of a couple of uncles who had considerately died within a year of each other, leaving him sole heir. It had not spoiled him. Good fortune never spoiled any body. It is bad luck that gives the devil his opportunity over men. At De Bacheville's I met the Marquise de Bellechasse, and sat beside her at dinner.

I think I had better not attempt to describe her. I have rarely known a beauty so vehemently attacked by women, so warmly admired by men. The source of her fascination was in her "general effect." So much so that I have heard two men who were equally infatuated with her dispute as to the color of her eyes. The quarrel was adjourned from the Jockey Club to the Bois de Boulogne, and the unfortunate fellow who swore by the brown eyes of his empress was carried home with a broken rib. The victor flew to the feet of the fair cause of discord to sun himself in the light of the blue eyes he had defended, and found them hazel. She seemed very tall, but was very little over the medium height of women. Her imposing air, her Juno-like walk, deceived every one. If her face had been faithfully put in marble, it would have been too cold, too strong. There would have seemed to be too much character in the traits. But no man could resist the strange, subtle charm of that soft, bright smile veiling in sweet and feminine beauty the fine firm mouth. There is not more variety in the myriad lights smitten out from a great diamond shaken in the sun than in the shifting expressions of her dark and unfathomable eyes. Like the mocking-bird of the Western woods they talked all languages but their own. They were too faithful ever to betray their mistress. It was her superb self-command that gave her command over others. Women instinctively felt this chilly empire over passion that she possessed, and took their revenge by small criticism. Men, beguiled by the music of her voice, the languid fall of the long, dark lashes over the vigilant eyes they veiled, the sweet smile that could seem so tired and dreamy, were conquered before they thought of defending themselves. Many a man thought on Monday, at the Tuileries, that this splendid woman was in love with him. He met her again on Tuesday at a Ministerial reception on the Right Bank, and was charmed and puzzled. The next night he went to the receptions on the Left Bank, expressly to meet her, and woke up Thursday morning restless and excited and alert, planning and scheming to see her again, in love and never dreaming it.

She concealed her youth as many women do their age. Her manner was that of a splendid young matron of thirty. But her cheek was infantine in its freshness, in spite of the gravity of the eyes. Her form was superb in the perfection and grace of its curves; but its lithe, and slender, and elastic beauty had all the indiscretion of a family record. It looked, as she was, twenty-two years old.

Though a good enough Christian in her way, she firmly believed in the unscriptural doctrine of hiding your light under a bushel. She was full of talent, but did her best to keep it out of sight. It hurts the self-love of men for women to be clever, and she did not care to add insult to the injury she did. So that few men knew that Adèle de Bellechasse read in five languages nearly all that appeared of value in art, and science, and history.

She was an American, daughter of what the newspapers call a Merchant Prince. A man enriched by sagacious trade. If he had enlisted for a soldier, he would have been a General. If he had drifted into politics, a Senator. He was a square, grave, witty, shrewd, well-bred man, with a bald head and a white mustache, who could drive his own bargains and his own horses, and buy his own books and his own wine, and who wouldn't be condescended to by a prince, if a prince were ass enough to try it. A man whom no country on earth but America could send out. Every where else it requires one lifetime to make a fortune, and three to learn how to spend it.

When Adèle Brinton was eighteen years of age she was driving in the Bois with her father one pleasant day. As they drew up by the Lake, a young fellow of about sixty-five, with suspiciously black hair, approached the carriage, bowed with stiff jauntiness, and began an aimless conversation with Mr. Brinton, for the purpose of staring at the pretty girl beside him. In a moment Brinton said, "Monsieur le Marquis, do you remember the little girl I had with me in Spain in 1852? Adèle, this is the Marquis de Bellechasse." The Marquis bowed with jaunty stiffness, and addressed his conversation to the late little girl. A week later he asked Mr. Brinton for the hand of his daughter. "Ask her," said the father, ringing for Adèle. She came in, fresh, and dewy, and bright, and stopped on the threshold, seeing the jaunty veteran again. "The Marquis has something to say to you," said Brinton, passing into his library. The astonished Marquis gasped out his prayer, all his jauntiness shaken from him by this unheard-of procedure. The young lady, not in the least astonished, listened with respectful attention and accepted with composure. "Come in, papa!" she called. Mr. Brinton entered, "*Embrasse ton fils,*" she said, laughingly, and left the two old gentlemen to talk business.

It was a perfect ménage. The Marquis made it the

study of his life to please his lovely young wife. Malicious people said he was faithful in that object "even unto death." He enjoyed his treasure only two years, and left his name and great wealth to his widow. At the time of his death he was Ambassador at the Court of—well, these are critical times for kings, we will say the King of Thule. Adèle had a great success in that witty, polished, and brilliant court. The gayest and the gravest were alike at her feet. Young Hussars littered her hotel with anonymous bouquets, and old savants made homage to her of ponderous treatises on the Origin of Matter. She left them all disconsolate—the periodicals of Thule were crammed with verses of farewell—she received from twenty admirers the highly original and suggestive cadeau of a bouquet of *Vergiss-mein-nicht*—and there was not beer enough in the kingdom to drown the despair of the *Junkerpartei*. She came down to Paris. She induced her father to take a floor of her hotel, and she accomplished discreetly her year of widowhood. Then she appeared again in the world, and Paris—I mean the few hundreds who call themselves Paris—was in emotion, like the waves of the sea when the full moon wakes them from their sleep, and they scuffle to gain one instant of her gilding light.

"The first thing the Marquise said to me, as we took our places at the table, was, 'Who was that in your window yesterday?'"

"My friend Cabell; but you know him?"

"Yes," she said, hesitatingly. "How do you know I know him? What did he say about me?"

"Nothing. Tell me what you know of Cabell."

"Answer *me!*"

"Really, it is because Cabell said nothing about you that I am curious to know what your acquaintance has been."

"I don't like to give something for nothing. Tell me all you know about him, and then I will take your question into consideration."

I gave her in brief an account of my acquaintance with Shelby Cabell. It lasted, with her interruptions and questions, from fish to finger-bowls, and she had told me nothing. The ladies went to the drawing-room and the men staid behind with De Bacheville, to drink a punch of Bourbon whisky, an old Washington habit of his.

When we joined the ladies Madame de Bellechasse, with the pretty imperiousness that was natural to her, ordered me to take what I could rescue of her sofa from the deluge of her toilet. She began to speak of Cabell in a confidential manner, which at once rendered me the envy of all the Frenchmen there, who could not dream of any thing but a flirtation couched in a semi-tone and a foreign language.

I was usually ranked among the victims of Madame de Bellechasse. I saw a good deal of her. I was very much attached to her father. They were both very kind to me. I believe the only thing Adèle saw in me that was worth her respect was that I did not love her, and did not flatter her. This was something phenomenal in her experience of men. It gave her a disproportionate confidence in me. She told me more than any one else, I believe. She thought aloud in my company. I was very much interested in her. But I was more in love with the Venus of Milo than with Adèle de Bellechasse, and with a better chance of a return.

I have said all this to explain how I came to know the story of Shelby Cabell's love. Adèle told me of it lightly and mirthfully, as she told me of a dozen declarations she had received in a week. She had grown utterly skeptical on the subject of genuine passion. Her endless "successes" had brought her to this. She saw few men she respected. She had never for an instant loved. So far as that god was concerned she was an Atheist. Her lovers filed before her like an unreal pageant, constructed for her amusement. She could not think of any thing real behind the scenes.

Yet even in talking of Cabell she seemed haunted by a vague suspicion that this man loved her. She did not care for him, and would not marry him if she loved him, she frankly said. But she would be sorry not to know beyond a doubt if she were really loved once in her lifetime. "He talked very much like the rest, but with less parade of passion," she said, finishing her story, "and when I said I would be glad to see him often as a friend, he smiled and said I did not know what I was talking about. I like a little rudeness in such circumstances. Altogether, his manner impressed me a little, and that is why I remembered his face, and asked you about him."

"I believe that Shelby Cabell loves you well enough to die of it some day."

"*C'est un peu fort ça?*"

She was always unusually heartless when she dropped into French. So I rose and went my way.

I have no heart to repeat the story she told me. It resolves itself into this. Cabell saw her one night in a Bal Masqué in Thule. The King himself had asked her to personate his kingdom. She marched at the head of a cortége, representing the nations of the world. She had a walk, in those great ceremonial occasions, that was worthy of the Kemble family. *Incedo regina* she could say if any could. Cabell was dazzled. He was presented to her, and was dragged for a while at her chariot-wheels. When she came to Paris he passed her, and a year before he declared his love; and with the unreasoning presumption of all true passion he claimed her love in return. She refused him as she would have refused a porcelain vase to a child who cried for it.

For her it was the amusement of a half hour. For him it was Life against Death. A thousand to one on Death.

From that night I was a prey to inquietude on Cabell's account. I had the key to his riddle. He affronted death with that utter calmness I had thought affectation, because he had no good reason for living. In the agony of his first despair he had resolved to die; and during the long months that followed he had grown so familiar with the idea of violent death, that it had become the settled habit of his mind to think of "dying in his boots," as they phrase it in the West, just as other people think vaguely of dying, ages hence, in bed. I could not call him insane. He was enthusiastic on the subject of artistic suicides; but the mania of a gambler or a turfist was no less incomprehensible and often far more hurtful. I remembered all the old saws against suicide, and used them desperately on him. But his reasons for, I felt, were stronger than mine against, in their effect upon a mind and a nature like his.

One day he said, "Suicide is generally considered the result of insanity. You have said so even. Tell me, do you think a man who coolly throws away a life that is useless and tiresome is as crazy as one who sacrifices in a duel a life full of pleasures and hopes and duties? Yet you call one act madness, and the other a necessary regard for the opinion of mankind."

I was silent, for I had been silly enough to say that. I thought if I could get him away from Paris I could cheat him by degrees out of his purpose. But he would not leave the city. He said that he intended to live as long as his money lasted, and he could not afford to travel. "My mind once made up to 'go off,'" he reasoned, "I am satisfied and happy enough for the few days that remain. The world has ceased to trouble me. I look on myself as a dead man, and have a foretaste of the delights of the grave. I am like a prisoner who will be free next week, and begins to be interested in the daily life of the jail, which was horrible before he heard of his pardon, and would be again if his pardon were withdrawn."

We were smoking one afternoon in the garden of the Luxembourg. A little child ran up to Cabell and kissed his hand.

"*Ça va toujours bien, ma petite?*" he said, kindly.

"Oh yes!" she said, "and we all pray for you every night, though papa says such a great gentleman does not want our prayers."

"Papa is wrong. I want them very much. Don't forget!"

"*Jamais*," said the little one, as she ran back to her brother.

"That expansive juvenile makes me remember that I am going off sooner than I had intended," he said.

"What has happened?" I asked.

He had filled his mouth with an enormous volume of smoke. Two thin blue lines crept out of his nostrils over his mustache, were caught by the undertow and dragged into his mouth. The tortured smoke came slowly out of his lips, and was in turn captured and drawn into his nostrils. A moment more he opened his mouth, and the balsamic vapor shot out all at once like burned powder from a cannon, and curled slowly up into the withering foliage of the elms. I was so lost in admiration of this elaborate master-piece of pneumatics that I forgot his story.

"Where did you accumulate all that science?"

"I got it," he said, "from a fellow in the Overland Pony Express. But I was going to tell you something else. What was it? Oh yes! I heard last week of a poor wretch who made up his mind, if he had one, to lay his head under a trip-hammer in an iron-rolling establishment. Not a bad idea, either. But the poor creature's heart failed him when he got by the side of the vast monster, beating on its quivering anvil with the force of a regiment of vulcans fused into a single arm. So he thought he would begin with his fist. It was a hard, horny, proletarian fist, but the smooth, shining face of the iron came down and flattened bone and blood and brawn out into something like an unsuccessful buckwheat cake. Of course it did not hurt him in the least, the whole nervous system being too much shocked to feel. He stood staring with the amused face of a stupid child at what was left of his hand until they carried him home. I remembered his address, and it caught my eye as I walked through the Rue Mouffetard a few days ago. I thought I would go up and talk with him. I might get some useful new idea out of him. I introduced myself as a Visitor of the Poor. Two or three frightened and ragged children crept into corners as I entered. His wife was crying at the window. I could make nothing of the poor devil: hunger and weakness of spirit had driven him into his folly. I talked with the wife and the babies. The woman seemed to have some grit. She had been a flower-maker; said she was sure of a living if she could raise 500 francs to begin upon. In three years she could save 4000 francs and set up a shop of her own. I thought, 'Here is a chance to do something. This poor woman is brave and industrious, and having brought those two little Gauls into the world, she ought to have a chance to continue her experiment with them.' I had in my pocket five notes of 1000 francs each, besides some odd hundreds. I had settled at Munroe's that day and drawn my whole balance. I gave her 5000 francs, and told her what my address was in case any body asked where she got so much money. I had the incubus of a husband carted off to the Hospital, and now every thing goes with them on wheels, as the happy creature says. She sits in her little shop all day at work at hideous roses and impossible coquelicots, which are bought as fast as made, and dreams of some day seeing her son an advocate and her daughter the wife of a notary."

"And does not this convince you that you have your work in the world to do? Seeking the happiness of others, you will find your own. These things always hunt in couples. Don't you see you have gained a victory over yourself?"

"A victory of Pyrrhus. Only it doesn't need another such to undo me. I have not the wherewithal for many more days. I am not sorry for that, however. This project of mine has been hanging by the eyelids long enough. So you need not be surprised to see me figuring before long in a *fait-Paris*. Good-day," he said, "I dine to-day *chez* Duval, and to-morrow—*Quien sabe?*"

I watched him moving off with his light, springing stride, graceful and free as an Indian's, and I would not believe so much life and beauty and strength was to be quenched. He turned at the first corner and looked back to nod to me again. The level sunlight was pouring its last rays through the dusty street, and I saw him in a sort of nimbus that does me good to remember now. It seemed to grow suddenly darker when he was gone.

I went home feeling very anxious. I was entirely powerless against his quiet, firm purpose, which had been cherished so long as to become to him a matter of course, neither to be questioned nor defended. Had I called him insane and asked for a "commission," any dozen doctors in Paris would have called me insane after the inquest. I resolved to play my only card. I still preserved the promissory note he had given me. He had paid the money long ago, but had not thought of his note.

I sent for a half-starved limb of the law whom I had employed in one or two little matters. Jacques Loup was a small, wiry, sharp-looking man, with a brown wig and the most remarkable eye-teeth I ever saw. They gave him a look of unutterable craftiness and malice. Yet the little man was as amiable as a sheep, and had no passions but for marionnettes and candied chestnuts.

I told him I would give him the full value of the note if he would put the debtor into Clichy within the briefest possible delay. I did not want the money; I wanted the body of the debtor.

"I see perfectly these have somewhat of mysterious there within. That does not regard me. I will impress myself to execute your vows."

Loup prided himself on his English. I could understand a good deal of it.

The next day I found Cabell's card at my house: he had scrawled on it "A little blackguard with big tusks dunned me to-day for that note I paid you. I kicked him a little. Was that right? Stole it, I suppose."

Poor Loup was having heavy weather, it seemed. I kept out of my apartment for a day or two, coming furtively in for cards and letters. I find another card from Shelby—"My little friend with the big tusks is suing me for that note. When can I see you?"

The evening of the fourth day I was in my parlor and heard a furious ring. I squared myself to meet Cabell.

But little Loup came tottering in. He was about to fall on my shoulder. I moved aside and he collapsed into an arm-chair.

"It is barbarous and savage, Monsieur, your debtor. I have execute your vows; but, *mon Dieu*, at what costly cost!"

He began to grow fearfully rhetorical and involved. I said, "Mr. Loup, your English is perfect, but a trifle too artistic for purposes of business. Please tell me in French what you have accomplished!"

This did not take long. The furious and blood-thirsty Cabell was in Clichy since noon. The process, though deeply interesting to Mr. Loup, would lack interest to the general public. I paid Loup his fee with a thankful heart. He went away, after expressing his firm intention, first, to *box* Cabell (whom he called Buveur de Sang) on the public streets; second, to fight him in the Bois de Boulogne, if Buveur de Sang could find a person *comme il fait* to serve as witness; third, to drag him before the Police Correctionelle for assault and battery, with intent not to pay his debts. All this, when the Honorable Monsieur Har-r-r-dang should be graciously pleased to let the blood-drinker out of jail.

I was almost happy that evening. I was sure of Cabell for a week or two, I thought; and I hoped to bring him to listen to reason before I released him. I had made up my mind to return to America if I could induce him to go with me. I felt so excited at the successful termination of my stratagem that I was too restless to stay at home. I looked at my cards, and saw that it was Madame de Rostainville's evening "at home." I went there. Madame was charmed to see me, and called me by the thirteenth name she had invented for me since our acquaintance began. I took it as a special attention until I learned that the Rostainville's *fort* was forgetting people's names.

The first group I saw was ranged around Madame de Bellechasse in various attitudes of adoration. I was lounging by, when she gave the word of command, "*Halte-là.*" I assumed the position of the soldier.

"Private Harding," she said, "will escort the Commandante to the lemonade. The Commandante is perishing with thirst."

But before we reached the buffet the Commandante forgot her thirst. Her infirmities assumed another shape. She was ready to sink with fatigue. Mr. Harding would lead her to a *causeuse*.

I was tempted to break my rule and fling myself at her feet. It would have been like the hundred millionth wave at the foot of Teneriffe, I know. But she was almost too bewitching for fallen human nature that night. Her eyes were dancing to a measure that Strauss would have lost his breath in attempting to follow. Her cheeks were ruddy as a child's. An impish spirit of mirth lurked in every dimple and curve of her lips. Her hair, which was trained down to the perfect brows, added to the effect. The great lady and the clever woman were gone on an indefinite leave of absence; nothing was left but the fresh, sparkling, intoxicating beauty.

Her first word startled me a little.

"Now hold up your head and answer; loud and distinct; you can't deceive me: what did you put your friend in jail for?"

This brought me back to serious matters "with a round turn," in nautical phrase. The thousand seductions which were wooing me to make a fool of myself sank into the background.

"For his own good?"

"How long are you going to keep him shut up?" The

brown eyes were dancing like mad.

"Until I can persuade him that a man can be happy and useful in this world, even without the smiles of Madame de Bellechasse."

This young girl was always a mystery to me. But to-night she was more sphinx-like than ever. What was she smiling at so strangely? What mirthful goblin was capering in the depths of her eyes? She wore that evening, over a robe of "illusion," out of which she seemed escaping at the top, a broad, bright cherry-colored scarf, tied like a belt so loosely that while one side of it was fastened at the slender, serpentine waist, the other side hung half-way to her feet. She frequently indulged in these graceful originalities, whose art lay in their apparent artlessness. She reached to the lowest point of this trailing cestus, and took from a pocket concealed there a letter, which she handed me, saying, "Read; and the next time you try to excite mutiny among my subjects, come to me, and I will give you some valuable hints."

This is the letter I read, Adèle's inscrutable eyes watching me, a dozen French eyes watching her, and the music wailing an air from the Traviata *Infelice*:

"Debtor's Prison, Clichy.

"Madame,—You once told me the best thing I could do was to go home. I was about to take your advice and leave Paris when I was arrested to-day for a small debt, at the instance of my friend Harding, who does not wish me to go. My preparations were all made, my means thus all exhausted. This debt is not just, but must be paid before I can go home. I owe one large debt, but can pay that after I am released.

"Please send me 300 francs by the bearer.

"Also,

"To-morrow, when you return from the Bois de Boulogne instead of coming into the Place de l'Etoile by the Avenue de l'Impératrice, I beg that you will turn off at the Rue de Presbourg and approach the Arch of Triumph by the Avenue de la Grande Armée. I will be where I can see you once more before I start on my journey.

"I ask of you these favors because I love you, and wish to be under some great obligation to you.

"You will grant them because you do not want my love, and will be glad to see me cured of it.

"Yours, even unto death, SHELBY CABELL."

"You understand this," I said.

"Perfectly. The man has a lucid interval, and is going back to Kentucky to 'reconstruct' himself. You have been frightened by his wild talk, and have put him under lock and key."

"You will not do what he asks?"

"Yes and No."

"You will not send him the money?"

"No, I will not," with laughing emphasis. "But I will make the whimsical détour to-morrow that he requests."

"He will not see you from the windows of Clichy."

"My poor dear friend, you are so delightfully stupid this evening. I said I would not pay him out, because I have done it already."

"Cabell is free?" I gasped.

"As free as you are. Freer, because you are with me, and I suffer no liberties in my presence."

This was said with a smile and a glance that would

have brought the Stylites from his pillar.

"Madame de Bellechasse," I said, "I fear you have done to-day an irreparable wrong. I beg you will not complete it by keeping that rendezvous to-morrow."

"Mr. Harding, you are growing tiresome. A gentleman as cool as you are in love-affairs should know that men don't slay themselves for honest women nowadays. I believe your friend Cabell loved me a little. I am grateful for it. I am glad he has recovered from his fancy. So I got him out of the Donjon-keep to-day, and I shall bow to him to-morrow with my best manner, as I roll in solitary grandeur up the Avenue of the Great Array. You will oblige me by calling *les gens de Madame la Marquise de Bellechasse*."

She passed out of the salon, nodding and smiling to the favored ones. I hurried over to Cabell's quarters. Of course he had not returned. His concierge told me he had left the house in the morning, with a man of the law, and seemed high in wrath. I passed my night plotting and confessing that plotting was useless. In the morning I determined to try the Police. I should fail, I knew. I should be laughed at, and if Cabell chose, I should be in greater danger of being caged as mad than my imperturbable friend. But I hoped to gain a day or two of time, and now that Cabell seemed out of my reach my head was full of the most unanswerable arguments against suicide. If I could see him I would overwhelm him with my powerful and novel reasoning. I obtained from the Commissioner of Police two *sergents de ville*, and in the afternoon we went to the Arch of Triumph. I gave them an accurate description of Cabell, and went with them to the top of the monument. He was not there. We descended, groping our way through the vast dark chambers, from one staircase to another. "How many doors are open to-day?" I asked the guard. "Only this." I placed my two sentinels on duty, and prowled around the vast monument, more at ease than I had been for many hours.

It was five o'clock, and already the refluent tide was pouring down the Avenue from the Bois. I was standing outside the great arch, on the western side, looking through the gathering haze to Neuilly, nestling on the right among the willows of the Seine; on the left the highlands stretching from St. Cloud to Mount Valerien, displaying its enormous bastions against the rosy sky. A paper pellet struck my hat and fell at my feet. I picked it up. It was a crumpled card. I read:

"Good-by and God bless you! I was in the dark chamber at the foot of the second staircase when you passed. I wanted to shake hands, but circumstances over which, etc. Give my love to the Bear Creek Boys. Her carriage has turned down the Rue de Presbourg."

I looked up. He was standing on the verge of the monument. He bowed and smiled.

I shouted to my policemen, "*Le voilà, là-haut!*" They rushed at the stairs. I turned and saw the Daumont of Madame de Bellechasse flashing and clattering into the Place de l'Etoile. Adèle started from her languid attitude in the cushions and nodded graciously, with a smile like a burst of sunshine. I saw the smile fade into an expression of horror. She fell back, covering her face with her hands.

I heard a rush and a splashing crash behind me. I saw that my boots were sprinkled with blood.

Kane and Abel (1871)

"Don't go to Mabille. It is dreary and stupid. The women are tired and hungry—too well dressed to enjoy themselves, and afraid to laugh lest they crack their enameled surfaces. The dancers are cooks and barbers and shopboys, turning an honest penny with their heels. The crowd is English and Yankee and Russian—the dominant races, I admit—but you haven't come to Paris to see them. Come with me to the Prado, the last stronghold of the old Gaulish gayety, and see the youth of Paris."

The three young fellows stood in the gay gaslight on the asphalt of the Boulevard des Capuchins, in front of the Grand Hotel. The speaker—Mr. Blair Harding, Citizen of the Great Republic—without waiting for an answer, hailed a passing cab, and hustled his two friends in. He demanded from the driver his *numéro*, and directed him to drive to the Prado. He got into the vehicle, and they rattled away.

He carefully rolled up the paper he had received from the coachman, and threw it out of the window. Raising his voice to overcome the noise of the wheels, he said: "Always ask these rascals for their number, and always throw it out of the window. If you ask for it, he thinks you are posted, and will not overcharge. And, while I think of it, you must get out of that shearing establishment at once. You know French well enough, and don't want to pay two prices for the crippled English they speak there. I pass an hour a day, on an average, cutting Americans out of the Grand Hotel, and keeping them away from Mabille. Our people have too long kept the breath of life in those two vast swindles. You must go to one of two quarters, Bréda or Latin, and take a quiet apartment where you can have the 'comforts of a home.' If a man knows how to live in Paris, he saves half his money and doubles his fun. I spent nearly all my shekels learning, and now, when I see a sweet, fresh specimen, just over, exposed to the snares of the insatiable Gauls, 'my soul within me burns,' as Coleridge's loquacious seafaring man's did, to show him the ropes. I am almost prepared to state, as my theorem, that the pleasures you enjoy and the consideration you meet with are inversely as the square of your expenses."

"Then I suppose, by following your injunctions strictly, a man who has nothing can get rich on his economies here; like the two Mississippi River gamblers who began one night with a dime each, and before morning had won from each other a hundred dollars apiece."

"I see youth is vain and forward," rejoined Harding. "You are chaffing me in return for my sage counsels. Of course you will spend all you have, but I want you to get the worth of your money. A man can do that in Paris, if all the sands of Pactolus were his."

Mr. Harding went on in this loud didactic strain, as the *fiacre* rolled over the asphalt or bounded over the cobble-stones through the network of streets woven in the heart of Paris, between the Boulevard and the Luxembourg. His two friends listened with that eager credence that the newly arrived always give to the worldly philosophy of the Parisian of some years' standing.

There is probably vouchsafed to few men in a lifetime a more delightful emotion than the first view of Paris. We can scarcely think of that Imperial City but as an exquisite animate organism, full of beauty and wit and charm; more head than heart, and more temperament than either. You have seen women like that. They are universally and immediately admired—it is hard to say why, except, perhaps, that they insist upon it. They live for the world's pleasure, and so find their own. They may be dull in private life, but what of that? They have no business in private life. One does not look at Paris as a home. You would as soon think of being domesticated in a ballroom. The first thought that strikes an American on entering Paris some pleasant day is, that he is especially fortunate in arriving at that moment, and he runs over his calendar to see what festival it is. The sun is so sunny, the clouds are so frivolous, the showers are so spasmodic and mirthful, the architecture so white and airy, the streets are filled with people so gay and cheery, and so evidently delighted that you have come, that you make up your mind at once that this cannot last long, and must be enjoyed while it is going. After a while, you find it lasts about three hundred and sixty-five days in ordinary years.

Of course you soon forget this surface glitter. If you be of inquiring mind, as be all Republicans, born skeptics and deniers of the apparent, you will scratch the veneering of joy, and find the substance toil, and success, and failure, and misery, as it is under grayer skies and in duller ways.

But the two young fellows who are being led like lambs to the Prado by the veteran Harding, who is a Kentuckian aged five-and-twenty and a Parisian aged two, have seen no shadows as yet upon this brilliant scene. They arrived this morning, and have passed the day in a sort of dream, wandering aimlessly around the showy streets, admiring everything with the *naïveté* of children around a magic lantern.

I may as well tell you now who they are. There is time enough. It is a long drive from the Grand Hotel to the Prado.

They are twin-brothers, named Kane and Abel Lennard, from East Barrington, Mass. Some two dozen years ago their father, Judge Abel Lennard, married Rhoda Kane, spinster, of that village. Both were well stricken in years. Judge Lennard had been married before—his wife had died childless. He had property in East Barrington, and, coming to look after it, he found an old memory of the singing-schools and sewing-circles of his earlier days revived by the pleasant eyes and voice of Miss Rhoda, who lived in one of his houses. The simple and wholesome life of the country had kept her fresh and comely beyond the wont of our early blooming beauties. The refusal of elderly suitors had become an ordinary incident in her quiet, happy life. She did not refuse the Judge. He never dreamed she had waited for him all these years. Perhaps she did not know it. But you and I, sagacious reader, know that the summer which young Lennard spent at East Barrington long ago, lived still rose-colored in her memory. The Judge seemed very slow to settle up his affairs. The matter of Miss Rhoda's lease and the conveyance of the land upon which her new house stood was especially puzzling to him. She would explain it to him fully one day, and the next morning he would come, as opaquely ignorant as ever. She wondered if all Judges were as stupid in law matters.

One morning she said, "Judge, this business of ours must be settled at once."

The Judge did not see the necessity of any haste.

"But I do. My year is out next week, and my new house is ready to occupy."

"Why go at all? You say this house is a very

comfortable one."

The Judge's manner and tone were anything but businesslike. As he spoke, he took the white, plump hand of his fair lessee, and to it addressed his remark. Miss Rhoda, though her attention seemed absorbed in a jay who was screaming in a maple by the gate, replied that the house was larger than she needed for herself and the servants.

"Then add me to your other servants, and let us all stay here."

The pink cheeks grew ruddy and the white hand warm and tremulous, but the sweet voice, still plucky and firm, said, always addressing the jay out of doors:

"Very well. I suppose that is the only way of settling the matter. You are *so* unbusinesslike."

So they were married, and their happiness was perfect when these two perfect children came. They were utterly alike; it baffled parental scrutiny to distinguish them. They were so identical in their babyhood that the fond mother used to call them "My son." But as they grew older they needed a name apiece. The widow Kane came in one morning to adore the infants in their double cradle. She was the far-away cousin of Mrs. Lennard. She asked their names. "They are not named yet." The good lady was scandalized. "Bring me the Bible," she said, "and we will see what they ought to be called."

She shut her eyes, opened the Holy Volume, and brought her withered index down on the page. It looked like a talon. One could imagine the texts crawling out of the way. "Now see what's under my finger." Mrs. Lennard read, not without a slight shudder:

And the Lord said unto Cain, Where is Abel, thy brother?

The venerable Puritan was a little shocked at the

response of her oracle, but soon recovered and valorously sustained it. "Those names will make them humble; keep before them a realizing sense of wickedness, and the necessity of brotherly love; better'n a sermon a day."

When the Judge came in the whole thing struck him like an epigram. "Why not?" he said to his wife. "Your name is Kane and mine is Abel. Couldn't do better by searching a year."

Mrs. Lennard was blonde and her husband was dark; so she gave his name to the fair baby and hers to the dark one. They had lost by this time their exact likeness to each other. Little Kane's eyes had grown dark, and his hair brown, and his brother had come to look like the conventional chubby cherubs, with golden hair and eyes blue as the deep sea.

They grew up handsome, hearty, brave, bright boys. They did their share of study in school hours, and played and fought enough to keep their young blood from stagnating, in hours of recreation. They inherited from both sides of the house unusual mental and physical vigor. They were not spoiled at home, though encompassed round about by a love intense and watchful as idolatry. For the love of the Lennards was veiled by the decorous formality that rules absolutely most respectable New England families. Thus had the Lennards, Judges, parsons, and soldiers, and the Kanes, parsons, soldiers and mariners, brought up five generations of reputable and God-fearing citizens. It was a sore trial to the old people to send the boys away to college. But they lived in a state of suspended animation through the terms, in the hope of vacation. When their studies had been creditably made, and the time came for them to see something of the world, their parents prepared to send them abroad, with outward gayety, but with a heaviness of heart too bitter to be entirely concealed. The affectionate sons saw that this agony was sapping the very life of their mother. They resolved to sacrifice their voyage, and informed her of it one bright day, alleging a new fancy they had formed to make an extensive tour throughout the United States. Her quick, sympathetic intuition could not be blinded. She forbade the sacrifice, and her fond gratitude gave her strength to kiss them smilingly good-by. They sailed away. There was a momentary wound of separation, which rapidly healed for them; for their minds were too full of hope to leave much room for memory. With those lonely ones at home life was all memory, and all hope.

They were boys to be proud of, if pride were not swallowed up in love. They were precisely the same height, weight and build—slight, but superbly muscular—a very little taller than the average. As statues they would have been identical—form and features being exact copies of each other. But the coloring and the expression were totally different. Kane had a clear dark *mat* olive skin; hair black, crisply curling; black mustache, that made his even white teeth flash like lightning when he smiled. And he smiled perpetually. Abel was blonde as a pure-blooded Visigoth in a straight line from Odin; gold hair, curled as if by the hot fingers of the sunshine; a mustache tinted like wheat, curving downward; and exquisite blue eyes, such as girls call poetical. He would have posed perfectly for an Adonaïs. But, in fact, he never wrote a rhyme in his life. Kane did, very neat verses.

I think no poem ever was written which could equal in lyric beauty and symmetry the double life of these young gentlemen—so perfect in youth, health, vigor and love. With their physical excellences they were sure to charm; they were rich enough to be free from care; they were clever enough to thoroughly enjoy.

As they enter the blazing vestibule of the Closerie des Lilas let us take one more view of them from another standpoint.

A thousand leagues westward—two elderly people are sitting in the twilight, talking of their treasures. At last the elderly lady says, "It makes me easy to think of Abel. He is so steady and wise. He will take care of his brother."

"Yes, he will take care of his brother," said the white-headed gentleman.

As Harding and the Lennards entered the vestibule, a medical student was quarreling with a policeman. The angry representative of the majesty of the law was vituperating in slangy French; the unmoved student was responding in fluent Latin, to the delight of his friends, and the confusion of unlettered tyranny. Tyranny, failing in the contest of wit, employed the arm of flesh, and marched off the young Hippocrates, protesting, in the purest Ciceronian periods, against such an invasion of natural rights.

"*Ex pede Herculem!*" said Harding. "That is the style here. At Mabille, the young fellow would have been better dressed, but his only arsenal of chaff would have been the *répertoire* of Thérésa."

There was a pause in the dancing. The musicians were mopping their fervent brows, and irrigating themselves with beer of Munich—a reminiscence of Vaterland. All Paris dances to German music; the time is more perfect in the solid Teutonic mind than in the more excitable Celtic, which is peculiarly sensitive to the charm of expression. There was a blaze of light more glaring than day in the vast hall. Under the splendid gas-jets wandered a company which could not be paralleled in the world. There are few things purely French left in Paris—

which, in becoming the rendezvous of the civilized world, has ceased to be the distinctive capital of a nation. But you cannot wholly Haussmannize the students of the Latin Quarter. Their joyous trysting-place is greatly changed in a half-century. La Chaumière is no more. The Prado has disappeared for ever from the Island, and in its place rises the pompous bulk of the Tribunal of Commerce. Centralization has attacked the gayest as well as the gravest of Gallic institutions; and the Prado, La Chaumière, Le Jardin Bullier, and La Closerie des Lilas, are one and the same—an immense dancing-hall, gay with gas, and brave with gilding; a garden fragrant with the faint breath of the lilacs, to which it owes its name; quiet alcoves for discreet conversation, and hundreds of little tables, where, in the happy French way, all the world refreshes itself in the sight of all the world. All is very fine and formal. The gendarmerie stand like gaudy statues around the hall and garden, useless and vivid. The waiters, neat and solemn, in white and black, seem always free from the wants and weaknesses of mortality. And the skeptical Yankees and bashful Englishmen go stiffly about, afraid to be gay. But nothing can utterly dampen the spirits of that joyous company, that still, in spite of the invasions and changes of the modern aedility, claim this place as their own peculiar rendezvous—sacred yet to youth and joy.

The night was fine. The hall was full. The garden was cool and dusk and confidential in the clear starlight—not too much illuminated. As the three Americans made the tour of the place, Harding spoke or nodded to many of the promenaders.

"It is the etiquette of the Closerie," said he, "to speak to the ladies without an introduction. Still, if you prefer, I will present you to any one you desire to know."

The Lennards hurriedly declined, alleging their imperfect French.

"Pshaw!" said Harding; "you speak like Academicians. I have not forgotten how you used to render existence hideous to old Leblond, at Cambridge, by your Odes of Horace done into Argot. How did you leave the old beggar?"

"Desolate," said Kane, "that he could not come with us. He said we would have a mad success in Paris—that he had given us the true accent of La Touraine."

"You must use it now. Here is a damsel from Tours, who will be charmed to hear the accent of her natal city. Nini la Tourangelle!" he said, stopping a rosy-looking girl who was sauntering by. "Here is a young gentleman who says you look thirsty."

"*Il n'en a pas menti, parbleu!*" frankly rejoined the young lady, taking the proffered seat, and calling for beer. "*Comment que tu t'appele, mon petit?*"

Abashed by these eminently easy manners, Abel hesitated an instant, and Harding answered for him:

"My friend's name is M. Thistlethwaite."

"*Mon Dieu!* these Polish names are enough to break all my teeth. Wilt thou dance?"

"I never learned," said Abel. "The *cancan* is not fashionable in Poland!"

"*Eh, bien!* you shall see me dance, and that will form you. Stand by that column till I bring my partner and my *vis-à-vis*."

"That is as good a place as any to see the dancing," said Harding. "Nini is rather famous. I will leave you for the present; I wish to speak with Cade Marshall, our Secretary of Legation."

The brothers took the places indicated. The quadrilles formed in a moment. Two long lines, reaching the whole extent of the hall—all sides and no ends; so that a set consists of two couples, not four, as in an ordinary quadrille. The Lennards stood just behind the Tourangelle and her partner, a tall, long-haired student, in tight trowsers, pea-jacket, and a slouched hat. The couple opposite had not yet made their appearance. Nini beat the floor impatiently with her little heels.

"*Mais depéche-toi donc, Rigolette!*" she shouted to a young girl who was chatting at some distance with a party of Englishmen. "*Voilà la musique qui commence, pristi!*"

Rigolette turned, and gave her hand to her partner, who was waiting for her, and the twain ran swiftly to their place. There was an immediate movement of the loungers in the hall to the spot where the set, thus completed, was standing. Kane and Abel, who had taken their places early, were, of course, in the front line.

A murmur of admiration ran through the crowd behind them.

"La Comète is looking superbly this evening!" "With whom is she dancing?" "Always with little Schnitzberg!" "Her hair is as prettily disheveled as ever!" "*Salut à la Comète!*" "*Vive la Reine du Cancan!*"

They looked at the celebrity thus apostrophized. They saw a young, but perfectly self-possessed damsel, with large gray eyes and good teeth; she was smiling an acknowledgment of the kind speeches that rained upon her—shaking out her neat and simple drapery, and pushing back from her temples the wavy masses of her pretty flaxen hair. Her partner was a strange stunted figure, broad-shouldered, with a sad countenance, small, sleepy eyes, and a nose of the Mosaic dispensation. She was of the medium height of women; he was scarcely so tall as she.

She was, on the whole, a pretty girl, neat and

wholesome. She wore a high-necked blue dress with a white collar; no jewels, plain red buttons at the cuffs and collar; imitation of coral, I suppose, two francs the set. The little man beside her was gorgeously arrayed in a green coat of a forgotten day, red waistcoat, and one of those astonishing hats that you never see without wondering what a low opinion of human taste the guild of hatters must have. He stood there, his long arms and great hands hanging heavily by his side, his face fixed, sad, only half-awake. But the instant the first blast of the music rang out from the orchestra, he came to life with a quick start as if shocked by it.

And all along the line of dancers life became apparent and alert. As the preluding strains died away, and the opening bars of the quadrille were played, the parallel lines came together and the *cancan* began.

The *cancan* of Paris is nothing but the conventional quadrille of the English and American *salons*. But it is the quadrille gone mad, the quadrille wild, disheveled, frantic. The same figures precisely as in the decorous dance of the bourgeois parlor, but embroidered, overlaid and hid out of sight by the most luxuriant and fantastic variations. It is rather a fantasia composed upon the quadrille as a theme. Viewed as a whole, it is a bewildering chaos of whirling figures, fluttering draperies, dust, and rushing, roaring noise, mingled in tossing tumult, while above these living waves flash out continually white hands, and nervous, delicate feet, as if of struggling creatures whelmed in the furious tide of cadence and melody.

The Lennards stood gazing at the scene, at first a little confused by its wild and lawless *abandon*, but soon comprehending the law that really underlay and directed its movement. Abel having seen enough of it from one point, wanted to change his position and take a view of the *tableau* from the end of the hall. "No," his brother answered sharply, "I will stay here."

"Very well. I will come back when the dance is over," said Abel, and moved away.

Kane stood leaning against a column, gazing with the fixed eyes of a somnambulist at the *danseuse* opposite him. She was strangely altered in the last few minutes. The passionate blast of the music had transformed her. The orchestra was performing the "*Orphée aux Enfers*" of Offenbach, playing as usual at the casinos of Paris, with little expression, but with unerring time and fierce energy and power. It is music that goes into the blood and burns in the very veins.

Rigolette was all alive and thrilled with it. Her face was pale save a bright red spot in the cheek. Her eyes blazed under the half-shut lashes. Her whole form, full and symmetrical, moved in the music like a willow in the wind. Not languidly and gracefully, but with the intense, absolute possession of a Ménade. Her little feet pattered on the floor like rain, or flashed in the gaslight above her head, quicker than the hands of a juggler. She revolved in a whirlwind of her own drapery or dashed through the maze of dancers with that eccentric grace that had given her the name of The Comet. All this in perfect time; she seemed tossed about by the tumultuous music, like a feather on a chopping sea.

The music ceased for a moment before the closing figure. She stood quietly, as if waiting, not resting. Her red lips were pouted, her gray eyes darker, her head thrown forward slightly, her hands clasped. Her eyes full upon Kane Lennard as he leaned immovable against his column, still dreaming at her. He started and flushed at her glance. He was not the sort of man that young women look at indifferently. Her look of interest turned to one of surprise and pleasure. The music struck up, and she plunged into the dance again.

Kane was filled with a strange, sweet trouble. He had not thought of this girl as a human being before. She was the *cancan* personified—the spirit of the mad dance. She would pass away in a moment, so he was filling his mind with her before she went. But she had looked at him with a girl's personal eyes, and the situation was materially changed. The music clashed to a close.

Miss Nini of Tours, having intentions on more beer, turned and said to Kane:

"Cain! *Où est ton frère?*"

"How did you know—" he cried, but instantly reflecting that it was only a stray shot, he added—"that he was my brother!"

"That sees itself. You are loaves of the same batch. Only *you* were baked longest."

"Mr. Thistlethwaite will be here in an instant. He told me to offer you what *consommation* you would accept, you and your friend Mademoiselle Rigolette."

"Rigolette! my dear child! Come! Here is a Polish Monsieur, stuffed with money like a Strasbourg goose, who wishes to nourish thee and me, from mere Christian charity."

Rigolette came, laughing.

"And the name of monsieur?"

"Don't be indiscreet. It is a name no jaw that respects itself can pronounce without breaking. Let us drink monsieur's beer and let his *etat-civil* alone."

At this moment Abel came back. Nini ran to meet him, and said:

"Yes, thank you—beer—we may as well sit here."

Abel saw himself sacrificed, and was too new in Paris

to be brutal. So he paid for Nini's beer and listened to her good-natured chatter.

Kane, left with Rigolette, said, "What may I offer you?" in a tone as tender and respectful as if it was his heart and hand.

"A cup of coffee. You have lately arrived in Paris, have you not?"

"Yes. What makes you think so?"

"Your politeness."

Kane felt as if his heart had been wrung by a strong hand. A feeling of deep, pitiful tenderness was added to the admiration with which this girl's wild grace had inspired him. They sat talking, through the next waltz. She refused one or two persons who asked for it, saying to Kane, "I don't want a man's help in dancing. The only thing I dance is the *cancan*. Myself and the music manage that."

Kane thought her very pretty in repose. The long lashes shaded the gray eyes into an expression of shyness when she glanced at him—which was not often. She kept her regard demurely fixed on the floor. The profile was clear, and not without a certain refinement. The high-necked blue dress seemed exquisitely filled, from the slim waist to the white neck.

Little Schnitzberg came slouching up for his quadrille. She rose to go, then turned to Kane, and said, hesitatingly, "There will be another ball here on Thursday.

"*Au revoir*, then," said Kane, holding out his hand.

She gave hers with a smile, and Kane thought, with a blush. And the blush grew rosier and the hand softer and whiter the more he thought about it.

Abel came up and interrupted his reverie.

"Let us circulate a little, find Harding, and keep him

out of mischief."

The brothers moved arm in arm. Everybody turned to look as they passed. It made people happy to look on them and bless them. So true it is, that to those who have, much shall be given. Because they were rich, and beautiful, and young, and loving, and happy, everybody's blessing was ready for them.

When they found Harding, they were ready to go home.

"You must not go," said he, "until I show you the queen of the revel, *La Comète*."

"Show us *La Comète*!" laughed Abel. "We are her oldest friends; her Podsnap; and Twemlow. We watched her through a whole quadrille, and refreshed her with mild narcotics at its close."

"Young gentlemen," said the venerable Harding, as they passed out into the quiet night and waited for their cab under the shadow of Ney's marble effigy, "I think you had better go home. You take too rapidly and too kindly to Paris life."

"It all depends on the instructor," rejoined Abel; "you see the fruit of your half-hour's sermon coming over."

"I will give you the antidote going back, then. Here you are, *cocher*! Au Grand Hotel."

"Did you notice a rum-looking little rascal with her?"

"You mean my friend Schnitzberg?" said Abel.

"Most knowing of greenhorns! yes, I mean Schnitzberg. Since you know everything, perhaps you know he is a malignant little devil of a Jew hatter—"

"I thought so—wears the hats he can't sell—"

"Who in the *cancan* is simply sublime. Rigolette never dances with any one else; which is a little odd, because, at the Closerie, it is considered *mauvais genre* to keep all the dances in the family."

"What?" said Kane, suddenly; "do you mean to say that Rigolette is—"

"Madame Schnitzberg at home. The little hatter works all day to lay his day's wages at her neat little feet. It is thought he would take out his heart and roast it to a turn to present it to his beloved on a toasting-fork, if the gift might find favor in those wide gray eyes of hers."

"And she is good to the little child of Israel, and sage to the Gentile world?" asked Abel.

"*Credat Judaeus*," said Harding, sententiously, and began to talk about college and the class of Fifty Blank, and what had become of the pretty girls. "Never mind about the ugly ones," he said; "they always marry young and get good husbands." In talk like this, they came to the Grand Hotel.

"You must get out of this to-morrow. I will come and hunt quarters with you. Now aren't you glad you went to the Closerie?"

"Yes," said Abel, "and very glad I don't have to go again."

That night, as the brothers were talking over the evening, Abel repeated some of the droll observations of the Tourangelle. Kane laughed, but did not mention the name of Rigolette. He scarcely knew why he did not.

The next morning Harding came down and took them house-hunting. They found in the Rue des Ecoles a pleasant apartment of two bedrooms, *salon* and dining-room, for little more than they were paying for one uncomfortable room at the Grand Hotel. The major-domo of that colossal establishment bade them good-day with great austerity of manner, not deigning to nod his red-tasseled head. Harding's company was conclusive against them. His "cutting out" excursions were no secret to the management. They could only revenge themselves, however, by confiscating his cards, and telling him his friends were always out. He used to stride past the *concierge* with lofty scorn, and rove through the labyrinthian passages till he found the numbers he sought, answering the "What seek you, sir?" of the prim waiters, with a savage and strident "*Rien!*" that appalled them.

A day or two later, they were fully established and domesticated. There is no soil so kindly for the nourishment and adoption of exotics as that of the good town of Paris. There is no taste which may not in Paris find its full gratification. She turns her myriad faces to her myriad worshipers, and each finds in her the ideal of his dreams. She greets every man in the world as if she expected him. So the Lennards, who had never been separated at home, soon found themselves insensibly drifting apart in Paris. Abel had always been especially fond of political and historical studies. He began at once a conscientious and exhaustive survey of the civil institutions of the city, and amused himself by tracing the growth of the town through the centuries, starting from Notre Dame as a nucleus, and searching for the traditions of the successive walls still haunting the spots from which curtain and bastion and moat have vanished, in the names of the concentric streets. This occupation seemed a waste of time to Kane, who thought it much more profitable to lounge away his days in the Louvre and Luxembourg, or in the shops of the workers in bronze and gold. Thus they frequently parted in the morning to meet only at night. They usually dined at home, served by an *épicier* around the corner.

Thursday evening Harding came in and said, "Madame de Bellechasse is in Paris for a day or two, passing from Germany to the seashore. She says you are her cousins."

"She is very gracious to remember it," said Abel. "My father's first wife was a Brinton, cousin of Lorthrop Brinton, her father. We have letters to them, but thought they were out of town at this season."

"Technically they are not in town. But they would be very glad to see you. Mr. Brinton spoke very warmly of your father. He and the marquise asked me to bring you to tea at their house this evening. You had better come. They leave town to-morrow. You may not see them till next winter, otherwise. And they are the most remunerative people in Paris."

"Of course we will go," said Abel, "It is very kind of them to invite us so soon and so informally. I saw a portrait of the marquise in Boston, which was too beautiful to be like anybody."

"Wait, rash youth, till you see her. It is time to be off, too!"

Kane had been thinking, half-guiltily, for a moment past, of his rendezvous at the Prado. He did not want to talk of it, and he did not want to lie. He thought, "Dress— go to the Brintons'—talk 'common friends'—come back— undress—redress—go to the Closerie—can't be done between now and midnight." He sat perplexed, shaking ashes from his cigar.

"Wait one moment, till I *frac* myself," said Abel.

"Nonsense!" cried Harding. "From June to November there is truce to dress coats. Nobody is in town, and life is luxury in a shooting-jacket. You come as you are, or not with me."

Kane said to himself, "I can manage it."

They drove to the hotel of Madame de Bellechasse. Kane told the coachman to wait. Harding said, "Let him go. We will walk back. The night is very fine."

"It may change in an hour. *'Bien foi est qui s'y fie,'* in this latitude."

They were shown into a dim drawing-room, ghostly in its linen wrappings. A servant announced them, and in an instant a door opened, and the head of Lorthrop Brinton appeared, followed by the rest of him. It was a superb head—the head of a Yankee Plato. He came plunging cordially forward and said, "I am right glad you came. How is your father? I am glad to see you—both of you—though, after all, there is only one of you—in two different lights. Come into the library." He led the way into a jewel of a room, where, sitting drowsy in the mellow light, was Adèle de Bellechasse, whose young beauty was even then the talk of half the *salons* of Europe, and whose retirement since the death of her venerable husband had hung society with crape.

In a moment every one was talking with the ease of a family gathering, just toned enough by the strangeness to be graceful. Time goes rapidly when clever people are making each other's acquaintance; and Kane, hearing a silver hammer ring on a silver anvil, looked up, and saw a silver blacksmith straightening himself into position, and the hour-hand of the clock he was serving, midway between X and XI. He rose, said "Good-night" and hurried out. He tossed the driver his fare and said, "*Au Prado! Filez!*"

When he entered the hall, the dance was at its height. The air was full of dust, trembling and throbbing with the music and the cadenced step of the dancers. He made the tour of the hall, watching for the blue dress he remembered. He did not see it. He took the seat he had occupied the first night he was there. His fancy created her again before him, fresh and gentle. He was conscious of being a little ashamed of his position. He did not know why he had come. She had probably forgotten him already. After all, he had better go home and not come back to the Prado again. It was amusing, this study of character, but not entirely reputable. He would not talk to Abel about it—therefore he ought to drop it. This was the delicate touchstone he had for years applied to all his projects.

He felt a light tap on his shoulder and a merry voice saying: "Take care, young man! If you go on amusing yourself in this boisterous way, the police will have to take charge of you."

"*Bon soir*, Nini," he said. "Where is your friend, to-night?'

"Which friend? Everybody is my friend, and he is here."

"I mean Rigolette."

"Oh, she has captured a Milord. She is on his arm somewhere. She is learning French of him. He speaks the language like a native—of England." Kane felt indignant. He was now sure he had been foolish to come; he would go at once. But he looked around everywhere for the blue dress, on his way to the door. When he reached the door, he thought, as he was never coming back, he might as well take a more careful survey of the establishment, as something really curious and worth seeing. "These long-haired and queer-hatted students are Young France," he said to himself. "The wars, the works, the revolutions of the future are hidden somewhere in the chambers of their brains. The boy is father of the man. The difference between a French *émeute* and an American town meeting, is about the same as that between the Parisian *cancan* and the Yankee sewing-circle."

Just under these profound reflections ran vaguely

through his mind a current of thought like this: "I might have known better—though she looked as if she meant it—is that a blue dress?—no, it's purple—I will take a cup of coffee and go—"

As he sat down again to order it, when comparative ethnology, political currents, social puzzles, faded out of sight, and his ill-humor vanished with it, in a glad leaping of his heart as it said to him, *There she is!*

In the same neat blue dress and blonde hair and wide gray eyes—on the arm of a stiff young Briton, who evidently was uncertain whether he was a hero or a laughing stock, for the time being. But when she saw Kane, she dropped the arm of Milord, and ran up to him, stopping short, as if not sure of her reception.

"Sit down; I was waiting for you," said Kane.

This time he was sure she blushed—a happy, sunshiny blush, like a rose-colored smile.

"I am so glad to see you. Every one says *au revoir*, but no one remembers. You are so good!" she said, in her soft, low voice.

The deserted Englishman came up. She rose and thanked him for bringing her to her friend. She hoped she would meet him again.

"*Moa vouloir donner vous* beer," he insisted.

She thanked him and declined with quiet civility. He would have quarreled, if he had had French enough to do it with grace. But a consciousness of bad grammar bottleth up wrath. So he went away, with a bad opinion of the French people, and comforted himself by thinking of Waterloo.

The delicate flattery of the scene was not lost on Kane Lennard. If she had seemed charming to him before, she gained infinitely in his eyes by the neat way in which she had banished his rival. For, alas! it had come to that. In the few minutes gone by, he had been jealous. It is hard to say if jealousy precedes love, or only indicates it.

"Is your husband here this evening?" said Kane, remembering what Harding had told him.

"My husband! I have none, *Dieu merci.* "

"But the Mr. Schnitzberg, who dances with you. I was told he was your husband."

"The world is mean and cruel. Poor little Schnitz! It is too absurd. He is old and ugly, and I am young and not ugly. We are not for each other. You do not believe that?"

"I am glad not to believe it."

"He loves me better than his own life, I believe. He came here and saw me dance one evening, and he looked like a man asleep—the eyes open. And often I saw him, always gazing at me. And at last he began to learn to dance the *cancan.* Figure to yourself how grotesque it was, with his shape. And he toiled every night, torturing himself to grow perfect in the dance to be fit to dance with me—as a monk tortures himself to be fit for heaven. And at last there is nobody in Paris who can dance as he can. You have not regarded him? But you must. He is marvelous. It is a rage. He is as perfect in his time as I. But beyond that, he is terrible. He is not himself, poor little Schnitz. He is love, rage, jealousy, despair. I sometimes get ideas from him. He would commit infamies for me."

"There he comes!" said Kane, as the shambling form of the Jew appeared in the distance. The couples were forming for the quadrille.

Rigolette turned, and said, suddenly:

"Do you want me to stay and talk with you, instead of dancing?"

It seemed to Kane that, even amid the keen pleasure which this suggestion gave him, a voice, almost audible in its distinctness, said to his conscience, *You had better say No!* So, after the manner of youth, he said:

"Yes!"

Schnitzberg came up, and held out his long, ape-like hand.

"You must pardon me; I am tired. Go dance with Nini!"

The color of the sad, sallow face was troubled a little, but without replying he walked away.

Kane called a waiter to bring coffee.

"No," said Rigolette; "it will be cooler and pleasanter in the garden after the dancing begins here—if you would like to go."

Again Kane heard that solemn, monotonous suggestion, *You had better not go!* He regarded it this time as a sort of impertinence, and said, promptly:

"I will go with pleasure!"

They went into the cool, clear, kindly night. They took an alcove in the garden, paved with small white sea-shells, and furnished with two rustic seats and a round marble tea-stand. It was completely walled and roofed by the dark-green foliage of climbing vines, whose faint, fine odors stole out upon the warm air of the midsummer night. Within the bower was fragrant and silent twilight. Without the gay garden, full of its joyous revelers; and just beyond, the vast open hall, blazing with light and roaring with the wild mirth of the dance.

"I did well to come," thought Kane, obstinately justifying himself. "It is a curious and instructive study of life and manners."

He looked across the table at the pretty young face framed in its wavy hair, resting on the small hands, with their neat white wristbands and red coral buttons, the red lips parted, the even teeth shining between them, and the wide gray eyes, that gave their own light to the face, gazing fixedly upon him.

"It was very good of you," he said, "to talk with me rather than dance, for you love to dance, don't you?"

"*If* I love it? It is all my pleasure in the world. I always loved it when it was only an amusement. But since I have had troubles, it has become a passion. When the first blast of the music comes, my spirit wakes up. The sound goes into my blood. My nerves tingle with it. I can feel the wind of it rustling through my hair. I give myself up to it, and the world fades. There is nothing but me and the music. The louder and harsher the orchestra grows, the better for me. I have often wished for a clap of thunder or an earthquake, to make more noise! And I am never tired."

"Then you lied to poor Schnitzberg?" (That sounds badly in English, but it is what one says in French.)

"Yes, a little. But truly, I did not want to dance. It is odd, but to-night I did not dance with *conviction*."

"Why?" said Kane.

She had not moved. The sweet face still rested on the little fists, and the great eyes, fixed as the pointer's, still shone wistfully on his face.

There was a little tremor in her voice as she said:

"I could not think of the music—for I thought of you— and hoped and feared—and looked everywhere for you."

The young man seized the little hands, and pressed them to his lips. When he let them go, she rested her face on them, just as before.

"Do you know why I wanted to come out here? I will tell you. In there, it is so bright and so public, one cannot stare long at another. They begin to talk and cackle. But here I may gaze at you, as I will, in silence. It is so good to gaze at you!" she said, dreamily.

Kane was greatly moved, but answered, lightly:

"Stare as long as you will; for, so, I have your face before me, and that is well worth while. You are beautiful, Rigolette, and—perhaps you will laugh at me, but I believe you are good."

The lustrous eyes grew suddenly dim with tears.

"Oh, monsieur! I love you for that! The good God bless you for that! It seemed to me you thought so. It is not for your beauty I kept you in my heart since that night; but because you treated me with respect, and I am not used to respect, and it breaks my heart with joy! No, no, monsieur!" she said, brokenly, taking Kane's hand, and pressing it to her heart, "it was not your beauty, though you are beautiful as a young god!"

A party of students passed by singing the refrain from *La Belle Hélène*:

> "*Evohé! que ces Déesses,*
> *Pour enjoler les garçons,*
> *Evohé! que ces Déesses*
> *Ont de drôles de façons!*"

She dropped his hand. "I will not compromise you. Good-by. You had better not come here much. I will never forget you. Adieu!"

She rose, yet seemed unwilling to go. She stood between Kane and the bright light of the garden. His artistic sense enjoyed intensely the graceful ease of her attitude as she leaned above him, resting one white hand on the lattice of the bower.

He thought of Latona's daughter, hovering luminous and loving over the most blest of shepherds, ages ago, on the dewless heights of Latmos. He said something of that kind. She looked pleased but puzzled.

She said, "Monsieur, do you really think I am nice-looking?"

She spoke earnestly, not at all coquettishly. Kane nodded and smiled.

"Then you will not be offended, I am sure," and she lightly stooped and kissed him. He felt her silken hair over his eyes an instant, and she was gone.

He went home, revolving many things in his mind. He said stoutly to himself, "I will not go there again." And she, before she slept that night, said softly to her own heart, "He will come again."

In the morning, Abel said:

"The fair marquise was a little annoyed at your abrupt departure last night. She said you were driven away by her Harmonious Blacksmith; that you started conscience-stricken as he began to hammer; that we were young in Paris to be watching the clock at that time in the evening—and remarks like that, in the piqued tone of a pretty woman who is accustomed to have men forget their engagements in her presence."

"She will forgive it before next winter."

"But they don't go to-day, as Harding said. They will be here several days yet. We are to dine there, *en famille*, Sunday evening."

The dinner was an exquisite one—only Mr. Brinton and his daughter, the Lennards, Harding, and Cade Marshall. Brinton liked young men, and they listened to his original, shrewd, and profound sermons with delight. The conversation was very vivacious: you will rarely find six people at table with so much to say, and so easy a way of saying it. Dinners in Paris in the summer-time are especially delightful. They have the charm of fruit out of season. Kane sat beside Madame de Bellechasse, who, coquette by instinct, thought it worth while to break a fresh Yankee heart, on her way from Baden to Trouville.

Her mourning dress, which was only a few months old, protected her from the dangers of flirtation, and yet heightened her young beauty so provokingly that it became at once sword and shield. She was witty, and wise, too, beyond the custom of beauties in general. So Kane chatted cheerily enough for an hour or so, while the delicate dishes and the faultless wines succeeded each other; and he thought, as the spirit of perfect content, resulting from a symmetrical dinner, diffused itself over his being, that his lines had fallen in pleasant places. As they rose, and went to the library to coffee, the Silver Blacksmith was banging ten on his precious anvil. The pretty widow turned laughingly to Kane, and said:

"We have you safe enough for this evening. The child of five generations of highly respectable Puritans can have no engagements after this hour of the Sabbath!" The sound of the clock, the marquise's mocking words, brought the image of Rigolette up before him, fresh, vivid, irresistible. It kindled him more than the wine he had taken. He had not dreamed of going to the Prado that night; but now it seemed that a thousand delicate fancies were wooing him to go. His eyes rested upon the fascinating face before him, but there was no meaning in them. He heard the ripple of her clever, sparkling talk, but answered vaguely and at random. A succession of pictures were passing before him—Rigolette in a tempest of white and blue skirts, whirling furiously through the cancan—Rigolette in twilight and tears in the garden! He could hear, ringing on his heart like the tinkling hammer on its argent anvil, her low, tremulous, passionate words. He must not run away first to-night, or he would fall under grave displeasure; so he talked on desperately until

Marshall rose to go. Kane said, "I will walk with you!" and made his hasty adieux.

He hurried to the Prado, and found her—gay and sad, wild and pensive—everything that a woman, loved and loving, can be, or seem to be.

When the brothers met at breakfast, neither said anything of the evening before. A faint, intangible cloud of distrust had arisen between them; the absolute oneness of their lives was at an end.

As I have said before, their different tastes attracted them, from the first, in different directions. Abel pursued ardently his historical studies, refreshing and amusing himself with archaeology. He did not see how his brother was gradually falling under the influence of an imperious and irresistible passion. Kane did not see it himself. He thought Rigolette was a most interesting specimen of a class hitherto unknown to him. He recognized her great charms, but thought he appreciated them aesthetically. He only hesitated for a moment, lest he should make her unhappy. But, with a boy's cynicism, he concluded there was no danger for her; and he could take care of himself. He did not know that weakness is infinitely stronger than strength, if strength is generous. He lay like a drowsy man in a skiff, drifting over sunny waves, through leafy, odorous islands, to plunging terror and death. He thinks whenever he chooses he can lift the oars and gain the shore in a moment. But the breezy river is better than the sultry shore, and the slight danger is pleasantly thrilling. When at last he is dancing on the breakers, and he hears the cataract growling like a wakening lion, it seems useless to row, and, with a heart throbbing with the wild joy of deadly danger, he rises to shoot the fall.

Several weeks after the departure of Mr. Brinton, Abel received from him an invitation to visit them at

Trouville. There was a postscript in the handwriting of Marchioness Adèle.

"If your brother will come, we shall be charmed to see him. I have left my impertinent smith in Paris."

"I would rather not go," said Kane. "Thank them for me, and say—anything—that I have friends here I can't well leave."

"You assume, then, that I am to go?"

"Yes—one of us had better, and I don't care to."

Abel went to Trouville. Kane drove to the station with him. As they shook hands in sober American fashion, among the osculating Alphonses and Alexandras, Abel said:

"I wish you were going."

"I wish you weren't," Kane replied.

"If it weren't silly, I would turn back now," said Abel. "I don't think we ought to be much apart. We are something more than brothers, it seems. I will not be away long. It will be rather a bore to write every day, but I will. Don't you fail. God bless you, boy."

"God bless you, old fellow."

Abel rattled away, grieved to leave his brother, until the frank welcome of Brinton, and the gay "*Bon jour, mon cousin,*" of Madame de Bellechasse made him at home in Trouville. Kane, as he drove back to his apartment, half-despised himself for the feeling of liberty that possessed and exhilarated him.

Dreaming and loitering, and utterly happy and content, Abel Lennard passed the warm, caressing days of the failing summer by the sea. On the golden sands, in the fresh tumbling surf, on the shelly beach, in the slanting daylight; and at evening in the thick, luscious shadows of Brinton's spacious garden; each hour came freighted with its quiet joys. He was young and strong, and the weather was fine, and Brinton was better company than anybody, and Adèle's eyes were the fairest that ever were so kind. It was the sweet Indian summer of his youth. Every minute of it is precious as his soul's life. For the storms and the frosts are coming, and then the long, dread days of ice and silence.

One morning, as Brinton, Madame de Bellechasse and Lennard were starting for a drive, a servant brought them a package of letters.

Adèle said, in a rapid, official tone: "I move the rules of common decency be suspended long enough to allow us to read our letters. Those in favor, read their letters. Those opposed, wait till the letters are read before objecting. Carried."

She tossed Lennard a letter, and her father and she divided the rest.

This was Abel's:

"MY DEAR BROTHER: I intend to be married in a few days. If you feel that you can trust my judgment so far as to consent to the marriage, I should be very happy to have you here. If not, I beg you will not come; for I am quite fixed in the matter. I am to marry Mademoiselle Marie Aucaigne, a sewing-girl. You saw her one evening at the Closerie—a pretty creature with blonde hair, who danced opposite us. Harding told us she was married— all *blague*.

"Her life has not been a very happy one; but she is still a mere child, and there is future enough for both of us. I marry her because I love her, as well as I can any one, and I know she loves me. After all, that is about the only thing worth living for.

"I know we Lennards have always been stiffish people in the matter of family pride. Perhaps it won't hurt us to take a recruit or so from the people,

"Dear Abel, trust me in this. If you can't congratulate me, say nothing. You will approve of my choice some day.

"Yours, affectionately, KANE."

The first few lines made him gasp, but he soon righted, read the letter through and put it in his pocket. He sat speechless with grief and anger.

"*Quelle horreur!*" cried Adèle. "Alice writes that Tom Webster has married his cook."

"Disgusting enough!" said Mr. Brinton. "I had heard of it."

"And then she adds, that she is a very good sort of woman—as if that was any excuse."

"No excuse perhaps, but at least some alleviation. Vulgarity may be reformed in the course of years. I think the only *impossible* marriage is one with vulgarity and vice. Death is a bad thing—but death is preferable to that."

The word sank into Abel's brain and staid there, and germinated into black and horrible, formless thoughts. He was pale and silent.

"You don't seem well this morning," said Adèle kindly.

He answered in a husky tone, as of a man who was tired with speaking:

"I am well—but sorry to leave you—my brother needs me in Paris. I must go by the first train to-day."

"You have no time to lose, then," said Brinton, and ordered the coachman to drive home. They saw he was in trouble, and forbore questioning.

Abel's spirits rose with the rapid motion of the train, as he sped on to Paris. A thousand schemes of escape and relief swarmed through his thoughts. He shut out from his mind the consideration of what he would do if the marriage were consummated. That must not be. That shame and disaster could not be. There had not been a discreditable marriage in the Lennard family in all time. There never should be. He would sacrifice his whole fortune to prevent this. If Kane would not listen to reason, he would buy off the vile creature who had entrapped him, by offering her more money than she ever had heard of. But he hoped to talk Kane out of his madness. He arranged it all neatly in his mind. He would get her out of the way. Then they would go to Italy and the East—and the old love and the old confidence would come back, and this day would only be remembered as a bad dream. He crushed his shame and fear under his feet, as the train went ringing and clattering on to Paris.

He arrived late in the afternoon, and hastened to the Rue des Ecoles. His ring was answered by—Schnitzberg! In black coat and white neckcloth, rigidly respectable.

"What are you doing here?" said Abel.

He? He was the valet of Mr. Lennard.

"And where is Mr. Lennard?"

He had gone out with madame.

Abel stifled a mad impulse to strangle the little Jew. Perhaps it was not so bad as it seemed. He would see if Harding knew anything about it. He drove to the Champs-Elysées.

Harding knew all about it. Kane was married three days ago, at the American Legation. There was no one present but the Minister and the Rev. Dr. Lambswool, who married them. Harding had learned of it through the parson, who was in a state of red hot enthusiasm over the bride's beauty.

"You told us she was 'Schnitzberg's wife,'" said Lennard.

"She was Madame Schnitzberg on the other side of the river. I did not say the Mayor had anything to do with it. But I beg pardon, Lennard; I can't talk with you about your s_____"

"Don't say that word, Harding!" Abel growled, in a dangerous tone. "Schnitzberg is there as Kane's valet. Did you know that!"

"Not possible! You must kick him out. My dear fellow, the thing is done now. It is absurdly melancholy. It rests with you that it shall not be too scandalous. You had better get Kane out of Paris. You may command me in everything."

"Thank you! People won't laugh about it long."

"You look very ill, Lennard. I know a good doctor in your quarter, if you need one." He was fumbling in his pockets for an address. Abel rose to go. "Here, you will find his name and address on this prescription, which I don't want."

Abel took the scrap of paper mechanically and held it clinched in his hand. As he walked downstairs, stumbling like a drunken man, Harding eyed him closely, then went to the window, saw him hail an open cab and drive off into the dusk of twilight.

"I will go over there this evening," he thought. "Abel is badly cut up. I am sorry I did not make him talk more. A little profane language would have relieved him."

Abel ordered his driver to take him by the Boulevard to the Place de la Bastille. He felt vaguely that he was not ready to meet his brother, that it might be better to wait an hour. He did not know his own purposes. He was dimly conscious there was something awful in the future: he wanted to keep it at arm's length while he rode in the cool air, and exhausted his invention in expedients. But he could not follow out for a minute a connected train of thought. A gust of passion and shame would scatter every plan to the winds before it was half arranged. The whole line of the Lennards, it seemed to him, was blighted and cursed. The past and future tarnished. As he passed by the Grand Hotel he drew his traveling *toque* over his eyes, and sunk back into the carriage out of sight, red with shame. He could see in the future nothing but ignominy and misery. Kane could not live abroad with this woman—all Europe knew her. He could not take her home among the pure and formal Kanes and Lennards. What then? Shocked at himself and fearful of his own thoughts, he burst into tears and prayed God to save him.

There are crises of morbid excitement where all the powers of the mind resume a kind of insane calmness and quiet, as of a stormy sea beaten flat by rain. The mind works clearly and actively, but abnormally. On false premises, it goes pitilessly straight to wrong conclusions. The conscience is silent, seemingly stricken dumb with terror.

Abel drew near the Place de la Bastille. He was confessing to himself that the disaster was irreparable; that nothing but murder could cut the complication; that this would simply aggravate the matter, infinitely increase the scandal, destroy both brothers and parents. In short it was not practicable: *if it were*—he clinched his hand anew; he felt for the paper Harding had given him. He had forgotten what it was.

"Where shall I drive?" said the *cocher*.

"To a lamp."

He looked at the paper. It was simply an order for a

vial of laudanum, which cannot be sold in Paris except by the prescription of a respectable physician. Harding had asked his doctor for it some days before, and had not used it.

His heart leaped wildly as he recognized the characters scrawled on the crumpled paper. With the rapidity of fever his mind dashed over the whole array of circumstances, and the vague and terrible fancy that had haunted him for an hour was instantly fixed into a definite plan for the rescue of his brother and the punishment of the Jew and the grisette.

"Schnitzberg has loved the girl—may be presumed to be jealous—every link of circumstance is perfect—and if there is any doubt, his Hebrew nose will convict him," he muttered, smiling grimly. In his mad eagerness to reach his object, these two lives seemed to him like cobwebs, to be brushed away. He gave the driver double fare and told him to drive—*ventre à terre* to the Rue des Ecoles. He felt as calm as a New England Sunday.

He found Schnitzberg at the door, who insisted on announcing him. There was a rustle of silk drapery, but when he entered, Kane was alone. They shook hands cordially.

"Where is your wife?" said Abel.

"She ran away when she heard you. The poor child was a little dubious of you. Let me call her back."

"Wait a moment. May I send your servant out for some cough lozenges? I am a little hoarse."

"Of course." Abel stepped into the ante-chamber and asked the Jew to go as quickly as possible to a drug store and buy a package of lozenges, and also the prescription which he gave him. Re-entering the *salon*, he was astonished to find himself very weak—scarcely able to stand.

"You look ill!" said Kane, anxiously.

"Give me some brandy!"

A liqueur-case was standing near. Abel drank two or three small glasses. Kane waited nervously for him to begin. At last, he looked up, and, seeing Kane's questioning eyes, said, with a smile:

"It is not worth while to talk about it. You know best what is good for you. We are all the world to each other, and we must not quarrel!"

Kane grasped his hands, and said:

"That's sensible, old fellow! You know you would not have consented, if I had not stolen a march on you. But she is the prettiest and sweetest and best—" and the enamored boy went on raving, in his happy honeymoon way, until his brother half melted. He thought, as Kane rattled on, what a fresh, frank child he was, so loving and true—what a hearty, brave schoolboy, quick and merry; he could feel his chubby arms around his neck, as if they were children together again, coming home from school through the shady lanes. He could smell the very apple-blossoms of the old times. The tears gushed to his eyes, for the second time to-night. Kane stopped his gay, hopeful talk with a look of pain.

"Never mind me," said Abel; "I am glad you are happy. I want this to be the happiest evening of your life. I feel that you are not altogether mine any more, and am a little jealous, I suppose. What are your plans?"

"We want your advice about that. I had thought of going home as soon as Marie learns a little English. She is very quick, and with both of us here, will pick it up rapidly. You will be delighted with her—" and again he went into loverlike superlatives about his idol, which Abel heard, but did not heed. He had begun to listen for Schnitzberg.

He asked his brother how the Jew came there.

"You remember, Harding said he was a hatter, and Marie's husband. He was as much one as the other. He was a valet out of place, and I took him at Marie's intercession. He seems devoted to her."

Abel was ready to die with pity for this noble, generous, trusting heart. Then he was possessed of a bitter, revengeful hate of the unworthy pair who, he thought, were plundering, after dishonoring, his brother.

"One crime—one punishment!" he said to himself, sternly.

His face grew rigid and hard.

He heard the outer door open, and went out. Schnitzberg gave him the packages. He put them in his pocket, first loosening the cork of the phial. Coming back, he asked Kane if he had some Burgundy.

"Yes, some has just come, that is called 'Forty-eight.'"

Schnitzberg gave them a bottle and two glasses.

"Give us three!" said Abel.

Kane's face grew radiant.

"You are the prince of good fellows, Abel!" he said, as the Jew filled the glasses. "Shall I call her now?"

"Yes."

Kane went into the adjoining room. Abel took up the glass first filled, and walked to the large lamp by the wall, as if to examine the color of the wine. He came back, and replaced the glass on the table. He handed the empty phial to Schnitzberg, saying:

"Take that out!"

The Jew did not look at it, but put it hurriedly in his pocket, as Kane and his wife appeared at that instant. There was not in all Paris a more charming and gentle-looking bride. Abel almost forgot his imminent vengeance, as she ran up and kissed him.

"It was so sweet of you to forgive us," she said, all smiles and blushes.

Abel hardened his heart, and thought, "My brother is worth saving."

Schnitzberg went to the table, and began arranging the glasses on a waiter.

"Leave that to me!" said Abel, sharply.

He took up two glasses hastily. He gave one to Rigolette and one to Kane; then, raising his own, he said:

"Bumpers to the Bride, and Welcome Home!"

All honored the toast duly. Kane made a wry face, and said:

"If that is the vintage of 1848, some of the bad blood they spilled that year must have gotten into the grapes!"

Abel burst into a wild shout of laughter, utterly disproportioned to so quiet a pleasantry. The others looked at him with surprise. He was of a ghastly pallor. Overcome by a sudden drowsiness, Kane dropped into a chair. Abel rushed forward, seized him, and raised him to his feet. He shouted hoarsely:

"Wake up! Look at me! Forgive me!"

The dark eyes opened—a gleam of quick intelligence flashed over the beautiful face. Rousing himself by an unutterable effort, he kissed Abel with an expression of divine compassion, and the twins fell, one inert mass, to the floor.

Blair Harding found them there an hour later—Kane quite dead, Abel in a deathlike swoon. Rigolette and the valet had fled in wild horror from the house, Schnitzberg snatching up as he went, to cover his full dress, a *paletot* of Kane's, in which he had left his *portemonnaie*. They were arrested a few hours afterward. The case was clear to any unprejudiced mind. But no French jury could sentence so pretty a head to divorce from such perfect shoulders, so Rigolette got extenuating circumstances. Schnitzberg paid the penalty of being ugly and a true lover. His attempt to fasten the crime upon the distracted brother of the victim caused a shudder of horror and indignation. And good-natured Paris had forgotten all about it (as Harding and Cade Marshall had kept the names of the parties out of the journals) by the time Abel Lennard lifted his thin, transparent eyelids from their sleep of feverish madness, and came back to this desolate world again.

The Blood Seedling (1871)

In a bit of green pasture that rose, gradually narrowing, to the table-land that ended in prairie, and widened out descending to the wet and willowy sands that border the Great River, a broad-shouldered young man was planting an apple tree one sunny spring morning when Tyler was President. The little valley was shut in on the south and east by rocky hills, patched with the immortal green of cedars and gay with clambering columbines. In front was the Mississippi, reposing from its plunge over the rapids, and idling down among the golden sandbars and the low, moist islands, which were looking their loveliest in their new spring dresses of delicate green.

The young man was digging with a certain vicious energy, forcing the spade into the black crumbling loam with a movement full of vigor and malice. His straight black brows were knitted till they formed one dark line over his deep-set eyes. His beard was not yet old enough to hide the massive outline of his firm, square jaw. In the set teeth, in the clouded face, in the half-articulate exclamations that shot from time to time from the compressed lips, it was easy to see that the thoughts of the young horticulturist were far from his work.

A bright young girl came down the path through the hazel thicket that skirted the hillside, and putting a plump brown hand on the topmost rail of the fence vaulted lightly over, and lit on the soft springy turf with a thud that announced a wholesome and liberal architecture. It is usually expected of poets and lovers that they shall describe the ladies of their love as so airy and delicate in structure that the flowers they tread on are greatly improved in health and spirits by the visitation. But not being a poet or in love, we must admit that there was no resurrection for the larkspurs and pansies upon which the little boots of Miss Susie Barringer landed. Yet she was not of the coarse peasant type, though her cheeks were so rosy as to cause her great heaviness of heart on Sunday mornings, and her blue lawn dress was as full as it could afford from shoulders to waist. She was a neat, hearty and very pretty country girl, with a slightly freckled face, and rippled brown hair, and astonished blue eyes, but perfectly self-possessed, and graceful as a young quail.

A young man's ears are quick to catch the rustling of a woman's dress. The flight of this plump bird in its fluttering blue plumage over the rail-fence caused our young man to look up from his spading: the scowl was routed from his brow by a sudden incursion of blushes, and his mouth was attacked by an awkward smile.

The young lady nodded, and was hurrying past. The scowl came back in force, and the smile was repulsed from the bearded mouth with great loss: "Miss Trudie, are you in a hurry?

The lady thus addressed turned and said, in a voice that was half pert and half coaxing, "No particular hurry. Al, I've told you a dozen times not to call me that redicklis name."

"Why, Tudie, I hain't never called you nothing else sence you was a little one so high. You ort to know yer own name, and you give yerself that name when you was a yearling. Howsomever, ef you don't like it now, sence you've been to Jacksonville, I reckon I can call you Miss Susie—when I don't disremember."

The frank *amende* seemed to satisfy Miss Susie, for she at once interrupted in the kindest manner: "Never mind, Al Golyer: you can call me what you are a-mind to." Then, as if conscious of the feminine inconsistency, she changed the subject by asking, "What are you going to do with that great hole?—big enough to bury a fellow."

"I'm going to plant this here seedlin', that growed up in Colonel Blood's pastur', nobody knows how: belike somebody was eatin' an apple and throwed the core down-like. I'm going to plant a little orchard here next spring, but the colonel and me, we reckoned this one 'ud be too old by that time for moving, so I thought I'd stick it in now, and see what come out'n it. It's a powerful thrifty chunk of a saplin'."

"Yes. I speak for the first peck of apples off'n it. Don't forget. Good-morning."

"Hold on a minute, Miss Susan, twell I git my coat. I'll walk down a piece with you. I have got something to say to you."

Miss Susie turned a little red and a little pale. These occasions were not entirely unknown in her short experience of life. When young men in the country in that primitive period had something to say, it was something very serious and earnest. Allen Golyer was a good-looking, stalwart young farmer, well-to-do, honest, able to provide for a family. There was nothing presumptuous in his aspiring to the hand of the prettiest girl on Chaney Creek. In childhood he had trotted her to Banbury Cross and back a hundred times, beguiling the tedium of the journey with kisses and the music of bells. When the little girl was old enough to go to school, the big boy carried her books and gave her the rosiest apple out of his dinner-basket. He fought all her battles and wrote all her compositions; which latter, by the way, never gained her any great credit. When she was fifteen and he twenty he had his great reward in taking her twice a week during one happy winter to singing-school. This was the bloom of life—nothing before or after could compare with it. The blacking of shoes and brushing of stiff, electric, bristling hair, all on end with frost and hope, the struggling into the plate-armor of his starched shirt, the tying of the portentous and uncontrollable cravat before the glass, which was hopelessly dimmed every moment by his eager breath,—these trivial and vulgar details were made beautiful and unreal by the magic of youth and love. Then came the walk through the crisp, dry snow to the Widow Barringer's, the sheepish talk with the old lady while Susie "got on her things," and the long, enchanting tramp to the "deestrick school-house."

There is not a country-bred man or woman now living but will tell you that life can offer nothing comparable with the innocent zest of that old style of courting that was done at singing-school in the starlight and candlelight of the first half of our century. There are few hearts so withered and old but they beat quicker sometimes when they hear, in old-fashioned churches, the wailing, sobbing or exulting strains of "Bradstreet" or "China" or "Coronation"; and the mind floats down on the current of these old melodies to that fresh young day of hopes and illusions—of voices that were sweet, no matter how false they sang—of nights that were rosy with dreams, no matter what Fahrenheit said—of girls that blushed without cause, and of lovers who talked for hours about everything but love.

I know I shall excite the scorn of all the ingenuous youth of my time when I say that there was nothing that our superior civilization would call love making in those long walks through the winter nights. The heart of Allen

Golyer swelled under his satin waistcoat with love and joy and devotion as he walked over the crunching roads with his pretty enslaver. But he talked of apples and pigs and the heathen and the teacher's wig, and sometimes ventured an allusion to other people's flirtations in a jocose and distant way; but as to the state of his own heart, his lips were sealed. It would move a blasé smile on the downy lips of juvenile Lovelaces, who count their conquests by their cotillions, and think nothing of making a declaration in an *avant-deux*, to be told of young people spending several evenings of each week in the year together, and speaking no word of love until they were ready to name their wedding-day. Yet such was the sober habit of the place and time.

So there was no troth plighted between Allen and Susie, though the youth loved the maiden with all the energy of his fresh, unused nature, and she knew it very well. He never dreamed of marrying any other woman than Susie Barringer, and she sometimes tried a new pen by writing and carefully erasing the initials S. M. G., which, as she was christened Susan Minerva, may be taken as showing the direction of her thoughts.

If Allen Golyer had been less bashful or more enterprising, this history would never have been written; for Susie would probably have said Yes for want of anything better to say, and when she went to visit her aunt Abigail in Jacksonville she would have gone *engaged*, her finger bound with gold and her maiden meditations fettered by promises. But she went, as it was, fancy free, and there is no tinder so inflammable as the imagination of a pretty country girl of sixteen.

One day she went out with her easy-going aunt Abigail to buy ribbons, the Chaney Creek invoices not supplying the requirements of Jacksonville society. As they traversed the court-house square on their way to Deacon Pettybones' place, Miss Susie's vagrant glances rested on an iris of ribbons displayed in an opposition window. "Let's go in here," she said with the impetuous decision of her age and sex.

"We will go where you like, dear," said easy-going Aunt Abigail. "It makes no difference."

Aunt Abigail was wrong. It made the greatest difference to several persons whether Susie Barringer bought her ribbons at Simmons' or Pettybones' that day. If she had but known!

But, all unconscious of the Fate that beckoned invisibly on the threshold, Miss Susie tripped into "Simmons' Emporium" and asked for ribbons. Two young men stood at the long counter. One was Mr. Simmons, proprietor of the emporium, who advanced with his most conscientious smile: "Ribbons, ma'am? Yes, ma'am—all sorts, ma'am. Cherry, ma'am? Certingly, ma'am. This way, ma'am."

The ladies were soon lost in the delight of the eyes. The voice of Mr. Simmons accompanied the feast of color, insinuating but unheeded.

The other young man approached: "Here is what you want, miss—rich and elegant. Just suits your style. Sets off your hair and eyes beautiful."

The ladies looked up. A more decided voice than Mr. Simmons'; whiter hands than Mr. Simmons' handled the silken bands; bolder eyes than the weak, pink-bordered orbs of Mr. Simmons looked unabashed admiration into the pretty face of Susie Barringer.

"Look here, Simmons, old boy, introduce a fellow."

Mr. Simmons meekly obeyed: "Mrs. Barringer, let me interduce you to Mr. Leon of St. Louis, of the house of Draper & Mercer."

"Bertie Leon, at your service," said the brisk young fellow, seizing Miss Susie's hand with energy. His hand was so much softer and whiter than hers that she felt quite hot and angry about it.

When they had made their purchases, Mr. Leon insisted on walking home with them, and was very witty and agreeable all the way. He had all the wit of the newspapers, of the concert-rooms, of the steamboat bars at his fingers' ends. In his wandering life he had met all kinds of people: he had sold ribbons through a dozen States. He never had a moment's doubt of himself. He never hesitated to allow himself any indulgence which would not interfere with business. He had one ambition in life—to marry Miss Mercer and get a share in the house. Miss Mercer was as ugly as a millionaire's tomb-stone. Mr. Bertie Leon—who, when his moustache was not dyed nor his hair greased, was really quite a handsome fellow—considered that the sacrifice he proposed to make in the interests of trade must be made good to him in some way. So, "by way of getting even," he made violent love to all the pretty eyes he met in his commercial travels—"to have something to think about after he should have found favor in the strabismic optics of Miss Mercer," he observed, disrespectfully.

Simple Susie, who had seen nothing of young men besides the awkward and blushing clodhoppers of Cheney Creek, was somewhat dazzled by the free-and-easy speech and manner of the hard-cheeked bagman. Yet there was something in his airy talk and point-blank compliments that aroused a faint feeling of resentment which she could scarcely account for. Aunt Abigail was delighted with him, and when he bowed his *adieux* at the gate in the most recent Planters'-House style, she cordially invited him to call—"to drop in any time: he must be lonesome so fur from home."

He said he wouldn't neglect such a chance, with another Planters'-House bow.

"What a nice young man!" said Aunt Abigail.

"Awful conceited and not overly polite," said Susie as she took off her bonnet and went into a revel of bows and trimmings.

The oftener Albert Leon came to Mrs. Barringer's bowery cottage, the more the old lady was pleased with him and the more the young one criticised him, until it was plain to be seen that Aunt Abigail was growing tired of him and pretty Susan dangerously interested. But just at this point his inexorable carpet-bag dragged him off to a neighboring town, and Susie soon afterward went back to Chaney Creek.

Her Jacksonville hat and ribbons made her what her pretty eyes never could have done—the belle of the neighborhood. *Non cuivis contingit adire Lutetiam,* but to a village where no one has been at Paris the county-town is a shrine of fashion. Allen Golyer felt a vague sense of distrust chilling his heart as he saw Mr. Simmons' ribbons decking the pretty head in the village choir the Sunday after her return, and, spurred on by a nascent jealousy of the unknown, resolved to learn his fate without loss of time. But the little lady received him with such cool and unconcerned friendliness, talked so much and so fast about her visit, the honest fellow was quite bewildered, and had to go home to think the matter over, and cudgel his dull wits to divine whether she was pleasanter than ever, or had drifted altogether out of his reach.

Allen Golyer was, after all, a man of nerve and decision. He wasted only a day or two in doubts and fears, and one Sunday afternoon, with a beating but resolute heart, he left his Sunday-school class to walk down to Crystal Glen and solve his questions and learn his doom. When he came in sight of the widow's modest house, he saw a buggy hitched by the gate.

"Dow Padgett's chestnut sorrel, by jing! What is Dow after out here?"

It is natural, if not logical, that young men should regard the visits of all other persons of their age and sex in certain quarters as a serious impropriety.

But it was not his friend and crony Dow Padgett, the liveryman, who came out of the widow's door, leading by the hand the blushing and bridling Susie. It was a startling apparition of the South-western dandy of the period—light hair drenched with bear's oil, blue eyes and jet-black moustache, an enormous paste brooch in his bosom, a waistcoat and trowsers that shrieked in discordant tones, and very small and elegant varnished boots. The gamblers and bagmen of the Mississippi River are the best-shod men in the world.

Golyer's heart sank within him as this splendid being shone upon him. But with his rustic directness he walked to meet the laughing couple at the gate, and said, "Tudie, I come to see you. Shall I go in and talk to your mother twell you come back?"

"No, that won't pay," promptly replied the brisk stranger. "We will be gone the heft of the afternoon, I reckon. This hoss is awful slow," he added with a wink of preternatural mystery to Miss Susie.

"Mr. Golyer," said the young lady, "let me interduce you to my friend, Mr. Leon."

Golyer put out his hand mechanically, after the cordial fashion of the West. But Leon nodded and said, "I hope to see you again." He lifted Miss Susie into the buggy, sprang lightly in, and went off with laughter and the cracking of his whip after Dow Padgett's chestnut sorrel.

The young farmer walked home desolate, comparing in his simple mind his own plain exterior with his rival's gorgeous toilet, his awkward address with the other's easy audacity, till his heart was full to the brim with that infernal compound of love and hate which is called jealousy, from which pray Heaven to guard you.

It was the next morning that Miss Susie vaulted over the fence where Allen Golyer was digging the hole for Colonel Blood's apple tree.

"Something middlin' particular," continued Golyer, resolutely.

"There is no use leaving your work," said Miss Barringer pluckily. "I will stay and listen."

Poor Allen began as badly as possible: "Who was that feller with you yesterday?"

"Thank you, Mr. Golyer—my friends ain't fellers! What's that to you, who he was?"

"Susie Barringer, we have been keeping company now a matter of a year. I have loved you well and true: I would have give my life to save you any little care or trouble. I never dreamed of nobody but you—not that I was half good enough for you, but because I did not know any better man around here. Ef it ain't too late, Susie, I ask you to be my wife. I will love you and care for you, good and true."

Before this solemn little speech was finished, Susie was crying and biting her bonnet-strings in a most undignified manner. "Hush, Al Golyer!" she burst out. "You mustn't talk so. You are too good for me. I am kind of promised to that fellow. I 'most wish I had never seen him."

Allen sprang to her and took her in his strong arms:

she struggled free from him. In a moment the vibration which his passionate speech had produced in her passed away. She dried her eyes and said firmly enough, "It's no use, Al: we wouldn't be happy together. Good-bye! I shouldn't wonder if I went away from Chaney Creek before long."

She walked rapidly down to the river-road. Allen stood fixed and motionless, gazing at the light, graceful form until the blue dress vanished behind the hill, and leaned long on his spade, unconscious of the lapse of time.

When Susan reached her home she found Leon at the gate.

"Ah, my little rosebud! I came near missing you." I am going to Keokuk this morning, to be gone a few days. I stopped here a minute to give you something to keep for me till I come back."

"What is it?"

He took her chubby cheeks between his hands and laid on her cherry-ripe lips a keepsake which he never reclaimed.

She stood watching him from the gate until, as a clump of willows snatched him from her, she thought, "He will go right by where Al is at work. It would be jest like him to jump over the fence and have a talk with him. I'd like to hear it."

An hour or so later, as she sat and sewed in the airy little entry, a shadow fell upon her work, and as she looked up her startled eyes met the piercing glance of her discarded lover. A momentary ripple of remorse passed over her cheerful heart as she saw Allen's pale and agitated face. He was paler than she had ever seen him, with that ghastly pallor of weather-beaten faces. His black hair, wet with perspiration, clung clammily to his temples. He looked beaten, discouraged, utterly fatigued with the conflict of emotion. But one who looked closely in his eyes would have seen a curious stealthy, half-shaded light in them, as of one who, though working against hope, was still not without resolute will.

Dame Barringer, who had seen him coming up the walk, bustled in: "Good-morning, Allen. How beat out you do look! Now, I like a stiddy young man, but don't you think you run this thing of workin' into the ground?"

"Wall, maybe so," said Golyer with a weary smile—"leastways I've been a-running this spade into the ground all the morning, and—"

"*You* want buttermilk—that's your idee: ain't it, now?"

"Well, Mizzes Barringer, I reckon you know my failin's."

The good woman trotted off to the dairy, and Susie sewed demurely, waiting with some trepidation for what was to come next.

"Susie Barringer," said a low, husky voice which she could scarcely recognize as Golyer's, "I've come to ask pardon—not for nothing I've done, for I never did and never could do you wrong—but for what I thought for a while arter you left me this morning. It's all over now, but I tell *you* the Bad Man had his claws into my heart for a spell. Now it's all over, and I wish you well. I wish your husband well. If ever you git into any trouble where I can help, send for me: it's my right. It's the last favor I ask of you."

Susceptible Susie cried a little again. Allen, watching her with his ambushed eyes, said, "Don't take it to heart, Tudie. Perhaps there is better days in store for me yet."

This did not appear to comfort Miss Barringer in the least. She was greatly grieved when she thought she had broken a young man's heart: she was still more dismal at the slightest intimation that she had not. If any explanation of this paradox is required, I would observe, quoting a phrase much in vogue among the witty writers of the present age, that Miss Susie Barringer was "a very female woman."

So pretty Susan's rising sob subsided into a coquettish pout by the time her mother came in with the foaming pitcher of subacidulous nectar, and plied young Golyer with brimming beakers of it with all the beneficent delight of a Lady Bountiful.

"There, Misses Barringer! there's about as much as I can tote. Temperance in all things."

"Very well, then, you work less and play more. We never get a sight of you lately. Come in neighborly and play checkers with Tudie."

It was the darling wish of Mother Barringer's heart to see her daughter married and settled with "a stiddy young man that you knowed all about, and his folks before him." She had observed with great disquietude the brilliant avatar of Mr. Bertie Leon and the evident pride of her daughter in the bright-plumaged captive she had brought to Chaney Creek, the spoil of her maiden snare. "I don't more'n half like that little feller." (It is a Western habit to call a well-dressed man a "little feller." The epithet would light on Hercules Farnese if he should go to Illinois dressed as a Cocodès.) "No honest folks wears beard onto their upper lips. I wouldn't be surprised if he wasn't a gamboller."

Allen Golyer, apparently unconscious in his fatigue of the cap which Dame Barringer was vicariously setting for him, walked away with his spade on his shoulder, and the good woman went systematically to work in making Susie miserable by sharp little country criticisms of her heart's idol.

Day after day wore on, and, to Dame Barringer's delight and Susie's dismay, Mr. Leon did not come.

"He is such a business-man," thought trusting Susan, "he can't get away from Keokuk. But he'll be sure to write." So Susie put on her sun-bonnet and hurried up to the post-office: "Any letters for me, Mr. Whaler?" The artful and indefinite plural was not disguise enough for Miss Susie, so she added, "I was expecting a letter from my aunt."

"No letters here from your aunt, nor your uncle, nor none of the tribe," said old Whaler, who had gone over with Tyler to keep his place, and so had no further use for good manners.

"I think old Tommy Whaler is an impident old wretch," said Susie that evening, "and I won't go near his old post-office again." But Susie forgot her threat of vengeance the next day, and she went again, lured by family affection, to inquire for that letter which Aunt Abbie *must* have written. The third time she went, rummy old Whaler roared very improperly, "Bother your aunt! You've got a beau somewheres—that's what's the matter."

Poor Susan was so dazzled by this flash of clairvoyance that she hurried from that dreadful post-office, scarcely hearing the terrible words that the old gin-pig hurled after her: "*And he's forgot you!—that's what's the matter.*"

Susie Barringer walked home along the river-road, revolving many things in her mind. She went to her room and locked her door by sticking a penknife over the latch, and sat down to have a good cry. Her faculties being thus cleared for action, she thought seriously for an hour. If you can remember when you were a school-girl, you know a great deal of solid thinking can be done in an hour. But we can tell you in a moment what it footed up. You can walk through the Louvre in a minute, but you cannot see it in a week.

Susan Barringer (*sola, loquitur*): "Three weeks yesterday. Yes, I s'pose it's so. What a little fool I was! He goes everywheres—says the same things to everybody, like he was selling ribbons. Mean little scamp! Mother seen through him in a minute. I'm mighty glad I didn't tell her nothing about it." [Fie, Susie! your principles are worse than your grammar.] "He'll marry some rich girl— I don't envy her, but I hate her—and I am as good as she is. Maybe he will come back—no, and I hope he won't;— and I wish I was dead!" (*Pocket handkerchief.*)

Yet in the midst of her grief there was one comforting thought—nobody knew of it. She had no confidante—she had not even opened her heart to her mother: these Western maidens have a fine gift of reticence. A few of her countryside friends and rivals had seen with envy and admiration the pretty couple on the day of Leon's arrival. But all their poisonous little compliments and questions had never elicited from the prudent Susie more than the safe statement that the handsome stranger was a friend of Aunt Abbie's, whom she had met at Jacksonville. They could not laugh at her: they could not sneer at gay deceivers and lovelorn damsels when she went to the sewing-circle. The bitterness of her tears was greatly sweetened by the consideration that in any case no one could pity her. She took such consolation from this thought that she faced her mother unflinchingly at tea, and baffled the maternal inquest on her "redness of eyes" by the schoolgirl's invaluable and ever-ready headache.

It was positively not until a week later, when she met Allen Golyer at choir-meeting, that she remembered that this man knew the secret of her baffled hopes. She blushed scarlet as he approached her: "Have you got company home, Miss Susie?"

"Yes—that is, Sally Withers and me came together, and—"

"No, that's hardly fair to Tom Fleming: three ain't the pleasantest company. I will go home with you."

Susie took the strong arm that was held out to her, and leaned upon it with a mingled feeling of confidence and dread as they walked home through the balmy night under the clear, starry heaven of the early spring. The air was full of the quickening breath of May.

Susie Barringer waited in vain for some signal of battle from Allen Golyer. He talked more than usual, but in a grave, quiet, protecting style, very different from his former manner of worshiping bashfulness. His tone had in it an air of fatherly caressing which was inexpressibly soothing to his pretty companion, tired and lonely with her silent struggle of the past month. When they came to her gate and he said good-night, she held his hand a moment with a tremulous grasp, and spoke impulsively: "Al, I once told you something I never told anybody else. I'll tell you something else now, because I believe I can trust you."

"Be sure of that, Susie Barringer."

"Well, Al, my engagement is broken off."

"I am sorry for you, Susie, if you set much store by him."

Miss Susie answered with great and unnecessary impetuosity, "I don't, and I am glad of it!" and then ran into the house and to bed, her cheeks all aflame at the thought of her indiscretion, and yet with a certain comfort in having a friend from whom she had no secrets.

I protest there was no thought of coquetry in the

declaration which Susan Barringer blurted out to her old lover under the sympathetic starlight of the May heaven. But Allen Golyer would have been a dull boy not to have taken heart and hope from it. He became, as of old, a frequent and welcome visitor at Crystal Glen. Before long the game of chequers with Susie became so enthralling a passion that it was only adjourned from one evening to another. Allen's white shirts grew fringy at the edges with fatigue-duty, and his large hands were furry at the fingers with much soap. Susie's affectionate heart, which had been swayed a moment from its orbit by the irresistible attraction of Bertie Leon's diamond breastpin and city swagger, swung back to its ancient course under the mild influence of time and the weather and opportunity. So that Dame Barringer was not in the least surprised, on entering her little parlor one soft afternoon in that very May, to see the two young people economically occupying one chair, and Susie shouting the useless appeal, "Mother, make him behave!"

"I never interfere in young folks' matters, especially when they're going all right," said the motherly old soul, kissing "her son Allen" and trotting away to dry her happy tears.

I am almost ashamed to say how soon they were married—so soon that when Miss Susan went with her mother to Keokuk to buy a wedding-garment, she half expected to find, in every shop she entered, the elegant figure of Mr. Leon leaning over the counter. But the dress was bought and made, and worn at wedding and *in-fair* and in a round of family visits among the Barringer and Golyer kin, and carefully laid away in lavender when the pair came back from their modest holiday and settled down to real life on Allen's prosperous farm; and no word of Bertie Leon ever came to Mrs. Golyer to trouble her joy. In her calm and busy life the very name faded from her tranquil mind. These wholesome country hearts do not bleed long. In that wide-awake country eyes are too useful to be wasted in weeping. My dear Lothario Urbanus, those peaches are very sound and delicious, but they will not keep for ever. If you do not secure them to-day, they will go to some one else, and in no case, as the Autocrat hath said with authority, can you stand there "mellering 'em with your thumb."

There was no happier home in the county, and few finer farms. The good sense and industry of Golyer and the practical helpfulness of his wife found their full exercise in the care of his spreading fields and growing orchards. The Warsaw merchants fought for his wheat, and his apples were known in St. Louis. Mrs. Golyer, with that spice of romance which is hidden away in every woman's heart, had taken a special fancy to the seedling apple tree at whose planting she had so intimately assisted. Allen shared in this, as in all her whims, and tended and nursed it like a child. In time he gave up the care of his orchard to other hands, but he reserved this seedling for his own especial coddling. He spaded and mulched and pruned it, and guarded it in the winter from rodent rabbits and in summer from terebrant grubs. It was not ungrateful. It grew a noble tree, producing a rich and luscious fruit, with a deep scarlet satin coat, and a flesh tinged as delicately as a pink sea-shell. The first peck of apples was given to Susie with great ceremony, and the next year the first bushel was carried to Colonel Blood, the Congressman. He was loud in his admiration, as the autumn elections were coming on: "Great Scott, Golyer! I'd rather give my name to a horticultooral triumph like that there than be Senator."

"You've got your wish, then, colonel," said Golyer.

"Me and my wife have called that tree The Blood Seedling sence the day it was transplanted from your pastur'."

It was the pride and envy of the neighborhood. Several neighbors asked for scions and grafts, but could do nothing with them.

"Fact is," said old Silas Withers, "those folks that expects to raise good fruit by begging graffs, and then layin' abed and readin' newspapers, will have a good time waitin'. Elbow-grease is the secret of the Blood Seedlin', ain't it, Al?"

"Well, I reckon, Squire Withers, a man never gits anything wuth havin' without a tussle for it; and as to secrets, I don't believe in them, nohow."

A square-browed, resolute, silent, middle-aged man, who loved his home better than any amusement, regular at church, at the polls, something richer every Christmas than he had been on the New Year's preceding—a man whom everybody liked and few loved much—such had Allen Golyer grown to be.

If I have lingered too long over this colorless and commonplace picture of rural Western life, it is because I have felt an instinctive reluctance to recount the startling and most improbable incident which fell one night upon this quiet neighborhood, like a thunderbolt out of blue sky. The story I must tell will be flatly denied and easily refuted. It is absurd and fantastic, but, unless human evidence is to go for nothing when it testifies of things unusual, the story is true.

At the head of the rocky hollow through which Chaney Creek ran to the river, lived the family who gave the brook its name. They were among the early pioneers of the county. In the squatty yellow stone house the present Chaney occupied his grandfather had stood a siege from Black Hawk all one summer day and night, until relieved by the garrison of Fort Edward. The family had not grown with the growth of the land. Like many others of the pioneers, they had shown no talent for keeping abreast of the civilization whose guides and skirmishers they had been. In the progress of a half century they had sold, bit by bit, their section of land, which kept intact would have proved a fortune. They lived very quietly, working enough to secure their own pork and hominy, and regarding with a sort of impatient scorn every scheme of public or private enterprise that passed under their eyes.

The elder Chaney had married, some years before, at the Mormon town of Nauvoo, the fair-haired daughter of a Swedish mystic, who had come across the sea beguiled by dreams of a perfect theocracy, and who on arriving at the city of the Latter-Day Saints had died, broken-hearted from his lost illusions.

The only dowry that Seraphita Neilsen brought her husband, besides her delicate beauty and her wide blue eyes, was a full set of Swedenborg's later writings in English. These became the daily food of the solitary household. Saul Chaney would read the exalted rhapsodies of the Northern seer for hours together, without the first glimmer of their meaning crossing his brain. But there was something in the majesty of their language and the solemn roll of their poetical development that irresistibly impressed and attracted him. Little Gershom, his only child, sitting at his feet, would listen in childish wonder to the strange things his silent, morose and gloomy father found in the well-worn volumes, until his tired eyelids would fall at last over his pale, bulging eyes.

As he grew up his eyes bulged more and more: his head seemed too large for his rickety body. He pored over the marvelous volumes until he knew long passages by heart, and understood less of them than his father— which was unnecessary. He looked a little like his mother, but while she in her youth had something of the faint and flickering beauty of the Boreal Lights, poor Gershom never could have suggested anything more heavenly than a foggy moonlight. When he was fifteen he went to the neighboring town of Warsaw to school. He had rather heavy weather among the well-knit, grubby-knuckled urchins of the town, and would have been thoroughly disheartened but for one happy chance. At the house where he boarded an amusement called the "Sperrit Rappin's" was much in vogue. A group of young folks, surcharged with all sorts of animal magnetism, with some capacity for belief and much more for fun, used to gather about a light pine table every evening, and put it through a complicated course of mystical gymnastics. It was a very good-tempered table: it would dance, hop or slam at the word of command, or, if the exercises took a more intellectual turn, it would answer any questions addressed to it in a manner not much below the average capacity of its tormentors.

Gershom Chaney took all this in solemn earnest. He was from the first moment deeply impressed. He lay awake whole nights, with his eyes fast closed, in the wildest dreams. His school-hours were passed in trancelike contemplation. He cared no more for punishment than the fakeer for his self-inflicted tortures. He longed for the coming of the day when he could commune in solitude with the unfleshed and immortal. This was the full flowering of those seeds of fantasy that had fallen into his infant mind as he lay baking his brains by the wide fire in the old stone house at the head of the hollow, while his father read, haltingly, of the wonders of the invisible world.

But, to his great mortification, he saw nothing, heard nothing, experienced nothing but in the company of others. He must brave the ridicule of the profane to taste the raptures which his soul loved. His simple, trusting faith made him inevitably the butt of the mischievous circle. They were not slow in discovering his extreme sensibility to external influences. One muscular, black-haired, heavy-browed youth took especial delight in practicing upon him. The table, under Gershom's tremulous hands, would skip like a lamb at the command of this Thomas Fay.

One evening, Tom Fay had a great triumph. They had been trying to get the "medium"—for Gershom had reached that dignity—to answer sealed questions, and had met with indifferent success. Fay suddenly approached the table, scribbled a phrase, folded it and tossed it, doubled up, before Gershom; then leaned over the table, staring at his pale, unwholesome face with all the might of his black eyes.

Chaney seized the pencil convulsively and wrote, "Balaam!"

Fay burst into a loud laugh and said, "Read the question?"

It was, "Who rode on your grandfather's back?"

This is a specimen of the cheap wit and harmless malice by which poor Gershom suffered as long as he stayed at school. He was never offended, but was often sorely perplexed, at the apparent treachery of his unseen counselors. He was dismissed at last from the academy for utter and incorrigible indolence. He accepted his disgrace as a crown of martyrdom, and went proudly home to his sympathizing parents.

Here, with less criticism and more perfect faith, he

renewed the exercise of what he considered his mysterious powers. His fastings and vigils, and want of bodily movement and fresh air, had so injured his health as to make him tenfold more nervous and sensitive than ever. But his faintings and hysterics and epileptic paroxysms were taken more and more as evidences of his lofty mission. His father and mother regarded him as an oracle, for the simple reason that he always answered just as they expected. A curious or superstitious neighbor was added from time to time to the circle, and their reports heightened the half-uncanny interest with which the Chaney house was regarded.

It was on a moist and steamy evening of spring that Allen Golyer, standing by his gate, saw Saul Chaney slouching along in the twilight, and hailed him: "What news from the sperrits, Saul?"

"Nothing for you, Al Golyer," said Saul, gloomily. "The god of this world takes care of the like o' you."

Golyer smiled, as a prosperous man always does when his poorer neighbors abuse him for his luck, and rejoined: "I ain't so fortunate as you think for, Saul Chaney. I lost a Barksher pig yesterday: I reckon I must come up and ask Gershom what's come of it."

"Come along, if you like. It's been a long while sence you've crossed my sill. But I'm gitting to be quite the style. Young Lawyer Marshall is a-coming up this evening to see my Gershom."

Before Mr. Golyer started he filled a basket, "to make himself welcome and pay for the show," with the reddest and finest fruit of his favorite apple tree. His wife followed him to the gate and kissed him—a rather unusual attention among Western farmer-people. Her face, still rosy and comely, was flushed and smiling: "Al, do you know what day o' the year it is?"

"Nineteenth of Aprile?"

"Yes; and twenty years ago to-day you planted the Blood Seedlin' and I give you the mitten!" She turned and went into the house, laughing comfortably.

Allen walked slowly up the hollow to the Chaney house, and gave the apples to Seraphita and told her their story. A little company was assembled—two or three Chaney Creek people, small market-gardeners, with eyes the color of their gooseberries and hands the color of their currants; Mr. Marshall, a briefless young barrister from Warsaw, with a tawny friend, who spoke like a Spaniard.

"Take seats, friends, and form a circle o' harmony," said Saul Chaney. "The me'jum is in fine condition: he had two fits this arternoon."

Gershom looked shockingly ill and weak. He reclined in a great hickory arm-chair, with his eyes half open, his lips moving noiselessly. All the persons present formed a circle and joined hands.

The moment the circle was completed by Saul and Seraphita, who were on either side of their son, touching his hands, an expression of pain and perplexity passed over his pale face, and he began to writhe and mutter.

"He's seein' visions," said Saul.

"Yes, too many of 'em," said Gershom, querulously. "A boy in a boat, a man on a shelf, and a man with a spade—all at once: too many. Get me a pencil. One at a time, I tell you—one at a time!"

The circle broke up, and a table was brought, with writing materials. Gershom grasped a pencil, and said, with imperious and feverish impatience, "Come on, now, and don't waste the time of the shining ones."

An old woman took his right hand. He wrote with his left very rapidly an instant, and threw her the paper, always with his eyes shut close.

Old Mrs. Scritcher read with difficulty, "A boy in a boat—over he goes;" and burst out in a piteous wail, "Oh, my poor little Ephraim! I always knowed it."

"Silence, woman!" said the relentless medium.

"Mr. Marshall," said Saul, "would you like a test?"

"No, thank you," said the young gentleman. "I brought my friend, Mr. Baldassano, who, as a traveler, is interested in these things."

"Will you take the medium's hand, Mr. What's-your-name?"

The young foreigner took the lean and feverish hand of Gershom, and again the pencil flew rapidly over the paper. He pushed the manuscript from him and snatched his hand away from Baldassano. As the latter looked at what was written, his tawny cheek grew deadly pale. "Dios mio!" he exclaimed to Marshall. "This is written in Castilian!"

The two young men retired to the other end of the room and read by the tallow candle the notes scrawled on the paper. Baldassano translated: "A man on a shelf—table covered with bottles beside him: man's face yellow as gold: bottles tumble without being touched."

"What nonsense is that?" said Marshall.

"My brother died of yellow fever at sea last year."

Both the young man became suddenly very thoughtful, and observed with great interest the result of Golyer's "test." He sat by Gershon, holding his hand tightly, but gazing absently into the dying blaze of the wide chimney. He seemed to have forgotten where he was: a train of serious thought appeared to hold him completely under its control. His brows were knit with an expression of severe almost fierce determination. At one moment his breathing was hard and thick—a moment after hurried and broken.

All this while the fingers of Gershom were flying rapidly over the paper, independently of his eyes, which were sometimes closed, and sometimes rolling as if in trouble.

A wind which had been gathering all the evening now came moaning up the hollow, rattling the window-blinds, and twisting into dull complaint the boughs of the leafless trees. Its voice came chill and cheerless into the dusky room, where the fire was now glimmering near its death, and the only sounds were those of Gershom's rushing pencil, the whispering of Marshall and his friend, and old Mother Scritcher feebly whimpering in her corner. The scene was sinister. Suddenly, a rushing gust blew the door wide open.

Golyer started to his feet, trembling in every limb, and looking furtively over his shoulder out into the night. Quickly recovering himself, he turned to resume his place. But the moment he dropped Gershom's hand, the medium had dropped his pencil, and had sunk back in his chair in a deep and deathlike slumber. Golyer seized the sheet of paper, and with the first line that he read a strange and horrible transformation was wrought in the man. His eyes protruded, his teeth chattered, he passed his hand over his head mechanically, and his hair stood up like the bristles on the back of a swine in rage. His face was blotched white and purple. He looked piteously about him for a moment, then crumpling the paper in his hand, cried out in a hoarse, choking voice, "Yes, it's a fact: I done it. It's no use denying on't. Here it is, in black and white. Everybody knows it: ghosts come spooking around to tattle about it. What's the use of lying? I done it."

He paused, as if struck by a sudden recollection, then burst into tears and shook like a tree in a high wind. In a moment he dropped on his knees, and in that posture crawled over to Marshall: "Here, Mr. Marshall—here's the whole story. For God's sake, spare my wife and children all you can. Fix my little property all right for 'em, and God bless you for it!" Even while he was speaking, with a quick revulsion of feeling he rose to his feet, with a certain return of his natural dignity, and said, "But they sha'n't take me! None of my kin ever died that way: I've got too much sand in my gizzard to be took that way. Good-bye, friends all!"

He walked deliberately out into the wild, windy night.

Marshall glanced hurriedly at the fatal paper in his hand. It was full of that capricious detail with which in reverie we review scenes that are past. But a line here and there clearly enough told the story—how he went out to plant the apple tree; how Susie came by and rejected him; how he passed into the power of the devil for the time; how Bertie Leon came by and spoke to him, and patted him on the shoulder, and talked about city life; how he hated him and his pretty face and his good clothes; how they came to words and blows, and he struck him with his spade, and he fell into the trench, and he buried him there at the roots of the tree.

Marshall, following his first impulse, thrust the paper into the dull red coals. It flamed for an instant, and flew with a sound like a sob up the chimney.

They hunted for Golyer all night, but in the morning found him lying as if asleep, with the peace of expiation on his pale face, his pruning-knife in his heart, and the red current of his life tinging the turf with crimson around the roots of the Blood Seedling.

The Foster-Brothers (1869)

One April morning, not many years ago, Mr. Cade Marshall, having nothing else to do for the moment, stood on his doorstep and looked at the Mississippi River.

It was not many years ago—yet since then a thousand glories and shames have dazzled and affronted the world; myriads of bright things have been darkened, and dark things brought to light; a continent has been dipped in blood, and has arisen from the red baptism cleansed of its deadliest sin. There is not a man now living who has precisely the same political ideas which he had on that April morning when Mr. Cade Marshall, idly enjoying the spring sunshine, looked from the door-step of his house on an Illinois bluff at the great river, and over it to the Missouri shore.

Mr. Marshall had been a Bachelor of Arts half a year. He had spent this time at home in the city of Moscow, Illinois, an ambitious town that had stretched itself so far over the hills and hollows skirting the river that it seemed doubtful whether it would ever knit its overgrown members firmly together. It had cut one hill in two, in the hope of a bridge which never was built. It had filled up one ravine, in preparation for a railroad which never arrived. It had a special charter from the Legislature, in case it should ever be big enough to need a city government; and it embraced several miles of the adjoining country within its corporate limits, to get taxes enough to keep up the expense of fire and lights for its Common Council. With its four or five thousand inhabitants it occupied about as much room as Paris, and sprawled over its half-dozen hills—as the elder Marshall once observed—"like a small but conceited hen trying to hatch a square yard of eggs."

A Norse poet mentions, as among the prerogatives of the gods, that they always look down. So the city of Moscow, sprinkled over its ragged bluffs, enjoyed much substantial comfort in looking across the river to where the city of Thebes clung with a precarious foothold to the Missouri mud—only existing by sufferance of the great river.

It was with a certain comfortable sense of superiority to fluvial accidents that Cade Marshall walked to his gate and glanced down the steep hill-path, two hundred feet fall to the water-side.

"The river is certainly rising," he thought, "and yet the *Lucy Bertram* seems to be stuck to the landing." But the steamer, which had been blowing and whistling, and ringing bells, and stirring up the yellow sand with her revolving paddles, now swung loose and headed for the Illinois shore, dancing coquettishly sideways over the water, keeping her head up stream. Two or three men with revolvers in their hands went shuffling by the gate.

"Thar she blows. Hurry up! Hi! or you won't fetch her."

"You bet I fetch her," answered a tall man with blue goggles. "Mornin', Mr. Marshall! Come along and help tie up the *Lucy*."

Mr. Marshall, much amused at being thus suddenly enrolled in the constable's *posse*, followed that functionary and said, "What has she been guilty of, Captain Ketchum?"

"Why, Jim Whaler missed his carpet-bag as he was a-comin' up from St. Louis, and he swears he believes the cap'n stoled it. I reckon he never done it; but that ain't my business. The cap'n offered to compermise by payin' for what was into it. So Jim he drawed out a list: one bowie-knife, one plug o' terbacker, one deck o' keerds, and two shirts. When the cap'n seed that he just sung out, 'oh, gas! Two shirts! when did you ever git two shirts?' So Jim he's got his back up, and he's took out a 'tachment, and we're goin' down to tie up the *Lucy* 'till they pay."

"Did you have the shirts, Jim?" said Marshall to the injured Whaler.

"I will, 'fore I'm done with 'em."

They reached the landing just as a deck hand came ashore to cast off the cable.

"Hold on there, my African brother," shouted Ketchum. The sulky Whaler stood by the rope, while the constable went on board and served process. Marshall went with him. As they reached the bar-room a youthful figure started up from near the stove, and a clear, hearty voice shouted, "Bless your dissolute heart, Occidental! how are you?"

Marshall started at the familiar college nickname, and turning, saw his friend and classmate, Clarence Brydges.

"*A la bonne heure!* Where is your luggage? Why didn't you tell me you were coming?"

"I am not coming. I am going to St. Paul."

"St. Paul can wait. Your boat is tied up. The captain and our constable will quarrel all day. You must go home with me. Give me your checks. 'False, fleeting, perjured Clarence,' to slip by without ungirding yourself beneath my roof-tree."

Brydges was soon convinced by the highly-seasoned discourse of the captain that his friend had spoken truth. They went on shore, and Marshall called a broad-shouldered, dwarfish German boy.

"Chris, take this trunk to my father's. Where is your cart?"

"I don't got none a'ready. Hans Doppelfritz his stief-vater gone dead directly, und mine gart is a funeral. I pack him selbst."

He seized the heavy trunk and trotted up the steep hillside like a mountain-goat.

Marshall and Brydges were preparing to follow, when Whaler rushed up, all the sulkiness gone from his hang-dog face.

"The cap'n's compermised. He agrees to pay for one shirt and treat the crowd. Come, take a drink, gentlemen."

At that moment a negro came running off the boat with a shabby carpet-bag in his hand. Whaler saw him, and grew sulkier than ever. He took the thin, leprous-looking bag of black oil-cloth from the porter, who bowed and grinned, vainly expectant of backshish, and slunk away muttering unorthodox expressions in regard to his "misfortnit luck." He disappeared up the sunken road to the town, followed by Ketchum and his friends, who made frequent and jeering reference to "them shirts."

The steamer, after expressing by emphatic growling and puffing her indignation at the "law's delay," went on her way up the river. The friends slowly ascended the hill to Marshall's house. This was a large, rambling structure, originally built for the block-house of Port Johnstone in the early Indian wars, with numerous additions and changes that had completely transformed it into a comfortable modern residence—as comfort is understood in the West—something very different from the Sybarite luxury of Fifth Avenue or the Back Bay.

"I am not sorry this happened," said Brydges. "There is no real occasion for me to hurry to St. Paul. I am making a rapid tour at the request of my father through the North. I have been reading some law in Mobile this winter, and the governor wants me, before beginning to practice, to see something of your country. You know he is a little *tête-montée* on this secession question. He thinks you will be a foreign nation in a few years, and he is anxious that I should see something of the present *régime*."

"Very well. Stay here and see it."

"But he insists on my passing all my time at representative places. St. Paul, as a north-west bastion of your power; Chicago, the home of the gnomes—the supernatural workers; Boston, your light-house; and New York, your 'ventral ganglion.' I have his positive commands against stopping for a day any where else."

"Except in case of accidents. We will prepare a new one every day until we fill a chapter, which we will send to your respected ancestor with our dutiful regards."

Coming to the house they found Mr. Marshall the elder sitting in his easy-chair on the long veranda. A fresh, rosy, black-haired old gentleman, who could even yet break a colt, or crack walnuts with his fingers.

"You are heartily welcome, Mr. Brydges. Don't stare; there is no second-sight in my knowing your name. That little Kobold Chris has come with your trunk, and I have sent it to your room. Will you go in, or stay here? When you are my age you will seize every moment of such lovely weather, and keep where there is most of it."

The young men brought chairs and sat in the soft spring sunshine. The impulse of awakening life was faintly visible on the bluffs, where the dry grass began to show an under-tinge of green. The warm light lay richly on the broad river and the brown leafless-wooded islands, and touched softly in the blue distance the high hills beyond the Missouri flats.

Brydges, who was looking at the town of Thebes, which lies in the delta of the Des Moines and Mississippi rivers, said, suddenly,

"What a quantity of ponds there are in that town!"

"Ponds that have come there since morning," answered Colonel Marshall, quietly. "If the river keeps its present mood it will sponge that town away in a few days."

"If you would like to see the village before the catastrophe we will go over after dinner," said Cade, laughing. "My father has so often prophesied the damp bad end of Thebes that we have come to regard him as a Muscovite Cassandra."

The Marshalls dined at the orthodox Illinois hour of one. Mrs. Marshall received her guest with the simplest courtesy, and made him feel instantly at home.

"I am never quite happy," she said, "when my table is three-sided. So you must keep that place, Mr. Brydges, till you are relieved."

The young men went down to the ferry in the afternoon and crossed over to Thebes. The river was tawny with mud and filled with the varied drift of the northern forests.

"The river is still on the rise, Captain?" said Marshall to the skipper of the *Osprey*, a long, silent, ruminant man.

"She's jest a-boomin'," said Captain Apple, increasing the volume of the stream by about a gill of nicotized saliva. "Five inches yisterday, and the big end o' that sence mornin'. The Dessmine is worse yet. Ef I was a rat in a cellar, I'd move up garret about these here times."

The *Osprey* came to the wharf, which had almost disappeared beneath the encroaching river. With that obstinate unbelief of the disagreeable that has been given us doubtless to prevent our suffering misfortunes in anticipation, the dealers in cord-wood were busy in removing large quantities of it from the waterline, and piling it a few feet further from the shore—to be moved again next day.

Marshall and Brydges walked through the town. It had been built before the levee, and so was on an average several feet lower. The side-streets and back-yards were therefore already invaded by the waters. A great quantity had come in during the night, creeping over the low banks of the Des Moines, and attacking the town in its unleveed and therefore defenseless rear. Many flat gardens and hollow commons were suddenly filled up with the muddy flood, as if it had soaked through the thin soil from below. A good many houses were built, with a sort of make-shift foresight, on detached piles. These stood clear for the present from the wet, looking like slatternly women holding up their draggled skirts. One dreary frame-house they saw where the piles had given way at one end, and the house stood helplessly with one corner in the air and one in the slough. They had the indiscretion to look in at the window nearest the road, and saw a sallow woman frying bacon at a stove lashed to the wall, and some ragged urchins in high glee climbing the sloping floor like flies, and sliding down again like musk-rats.

Everywhere a dismal air of make-shift. All the gates were tied up with ropes—the latches all gone. At the front-doors of several rather ambitious-looking houses a small ladder supplied the place of a porch. Many of the houses were unpainted, and looked prematurely old and shabby. Every thing seemed to say, What is the use? Dirty clay-colored curs lounged on the muddy door-steps with a dispirited and dejected air. The very streets, that started with fair prospects, seemed to grow discouraged and to flatten supinely out into bottomless black mud. The cats found it difficult to make their visits with any regard to neat feet. Long, gaunt, red-haired hogs grunted unsociably in the dry spots that were yet left them, too listless to be hungry.

In the best quarter of the town the two friends came to a large barn-like church with an unfinished steeple, around which the scaffolding was falling to pieces. Here the side-walk was elevated upon poles to the level of the fence-posts. This had been done some years before in the stress of former floods, and no one had as yet had energy enough to take it down. Turning its corner they found themselves before a larger and better house than any they had before seen. The garden before the door was completely submerged. A young girl standing upright in a light skiff sculled it dexterously about the garden with a long oar. It was a very pretty picture—the exquisite form swaying to every movement of the frail boat, the warm sunshine touching with gold lights the dark brown hair.

"Who has not heard of a jolly young waterman?" sang Marshall.

She turned, and with one stroke of the oar brought her skiff to the gate; she gave her hand to Marshall with a gay "Good-morning."

Miss Des Ponts, let me present my friend Mr. Brydges."

"Will you tempt the dangers of the deep and come in?" she said.

Marshall looked at Brydges, who eagerly nodded assent.

"You will come first, Mr. Brydges," said the fair mariner. "Mr. Marshall is *chez lui* in my boat."

She gave Brydges her hand to assist him into the boat. It was a soft white hand—"the hand of a marquise," Balzac would have said—with a firm and vigorous grasp. Arriving at the door-step she stepped lightly out of the skiff, and led her visitors into a cheerful-looking drawing-room carpeted in warm bright colors, richly furnished and curtained, where a brisk fire of hickory logs cracked and sparkled in the wide chimney.

"A fancy of papa's," said Miss Des Ponts. "He insists upon this open fire until the first of May, even if we have a torrid April like this. Cade, open the windows."

Mr. Marshall obeyed the peremptory order; then, in the same familiar tone, said, "Mimi, when are you coming over to spend the forty diluvial days and nights?"

"Silence, rash Muscovite! The river is merely performing its fertilizing office for the city of its love. It will be in its bed to-morrow."

"And to-morrow and to-morrow," added Marshall, tragically.

"I am ashamed to own," said Miss Des Ponts, "that papa has been carried away by the prevailing stampede. He wanted the furniture moved up stairs yesterday, but I fought hard and got a reprieve till to-day. I thought it would be a sort of treason to the river to distrust its honorable intentions."

"Pray let us hear your piano once more before it is banished to the attic."

She went to the instrument, and her fingers strayed for a moment over the keys, "building a bridge from dream-land." She then played with singular feeling and expression a low, solemn, dirge-like movement, which neither of the gentlemen recognized, but which was intensely thrilling and saddening. It closed with a sudden and startling discord, and she instantly broke into one of the younger Strauss's most Champagny mazurkas, which she gave with such grace and spirit that Marshall vowed he could see the flash of white satin boots, and catch the distant popping of corks in the supper-room.

Brydges, who had been somehow vaguely annoyed at the easy familiarity existing between Marshall and Miss Dos Ponts, had taken no part in the conversation. While she played he devoured her with his eyes. If she seemed lovely in the broad light outside, she was vastly more so now; her brown eyes softened by feeling, her exquisite lips slightly parted, a delicate tinge hovering like the first flush of dawn on the perfect pale cheek.

Her eyes lighted on Brydges for an instant as she played the last lively bars.

"I hope you will remain some time," she said. "I have heard Mr. Marshall say so much of you that I have been quite anxious to know you."

Brydges hardly knew whether to be pleased or vexed. This lovely, intrepid, self-possessed girl, treating him with this utterly unconventional frankness, was not at all flattering to his *amour-propre*. He jumped to the hasty conclusion that she must be *fiancée* to Marshall. He felt half inclined to hate them both. He hated himself worse for feeling embarrassed by the steady glance of the soft brown eyes.

"Yes—that is, not long," he stammered; then added, with unnecessary emphasis, "I am going to-morrow."

Marshall laughed and said, "Mimi, he will spend a week or two with us. Your music shall soothe his savage breast till we get tired of him and send him on his way, a sadder and a better man."

They rose to go. Miss Des Ponts rang, and a silver-haired negro answered.

"Take these gentlemen to the gate, Darby";" but,

glancing out of the window, she exclaimed, "No! voilà, papa! I will go myself."

As they sculled over the garden Marshall said, "Des Ponts translates Brydges."

"Not oversets, I hope, as Father Krakwity would say," she answered, laughing.

Mr. Des Ponts stood at the gate. There was a hurried introduction and word of greeting.

"My mother expects you every day, and hereafter we wait dinner for you," said Marshall.

Des Ponts looked troubled and anxious.

"I fear we *must* very soon claim your hospitality. This rise looks serious. The Des Moines is full of back-water for miles. The 'oldest inhabitants' are talking like screech-owls this afternoon."

"Never mind, *mon petit papa*. Here's a sigh for those that love us, and a smile for those that hate, and—and—before it gets above us, perhaps it may abate"; and father and daughter sculled to their beleaguered mansion.

As Marshall and Brydges walked to the ferry they saw evident signs of consternation among the towns-people. Those who lived in two-story houses were engaged in emptying their ground-floors, while the groundlings were begging room "under the shingles" from their more fortunate neighbors. Still, some esprits forts were walking calmly about deriding and pooh-poohing, and demonstrating by all the almanacs known that this "was not a high-water year."

That evening the young gentlemen were smoking on the veranda in the dim, confidential starlight. Brydges said, apropos of nothing: "Cade, I congratulate you. Miss Des Ponts is an excessively pretty girl."

"My dear Clarence, you have more taste than sagacity. I have no property whatever in Mimi Des

Ponts's unquestionable beauty."

"Why not?" rejoined Brydges, in a somewhat querulous tone. "You don't mean that there are more of that style of girls in the neighborhood; and whom, besides you, would *she* look at hereaway?"

"It is very sweet of you, gentle stranger, to say such things of both of us. Mimi and I love each other too well to be lovers, I suppose. I never had any sister but her; nor she ever a brother but me. We made mud-pies together, and fought over the first strawberries of the season. But I have never thought of availing myself of my evident advantages. I have magnanimously waited for some handsome pilgrim with blue eyes to come, and, if worthy and enterprising, to win her."

"Elle vaut bien la peine."

"*You* have the requisite Gothic complexion; you will have idleness and juxtaposition in your favor in a day or two. The great river is working valiantly for you to-night."

"What a superb picture of quiet power!" said Brydges. "There it flows, pouring out over the level bottoms the flood of ten thousand thunder-storms, annihilating farms, fields, and villages, and not the murmur of a ripple comes up to us in this deep silence. It was a true artistic thought of the old religions that made gods of the rivers."

"Yes. I think even Carlyle would respect the Mississippi—so much work with so little talk."

From the window of his chamber that night Clarence Brydges looked out once more upon the vast and broadening sheet of water, and the twinkling lights of the village by the shore. One, he fancied, without any reason except its brightness, was lighting Marie Des Ponts to rest. He gazed musingly at this light till it suddenly disappeared.

"Good-night, and happy dreams," he murmured; then added, "Well, I have given that dark-eyed Missourian enough of my thoughts to-night," and went on thinking of nothing else till he fell asleep.

In the morning, as he came out upon the veranda, he saw the Colonel gazing intently at something in the river. "Cade, my son, get my field-glass. Good-morning, Mr. Brydges. I hope you had pleasant dreams your first night at Fort Johnstone. You know they are to come true, according to our received traditions."

Cade handed him the glass. He glanced at the object that had puzzled him, and laughed—a hearty, strutting, crowing sort of laugh, and handed the glass to Brydges. "There, I don't believe even so blasé a veteran as yourself ever saw a sight like that before."

It was a chicken-coop floating down the river, its hapless inmates roosting on the roof with an air of draggled and desperate resignation. It was a slight but most significant specimen of the night's work.

"Look across the river, Mr. Brydges. The ponds of yesterday are lakes and bays. Behind the town the prairie is one vast sheet of water to the bluffs. Below us the Illinois shore is invaded; the bottom will be flooded to-morrow."

"We shall have the Des Ponts to dinner, doubtless."

"Yes; and then, Mr. Brydges, look out for your heart, if you carry any such light baggage."

The theme was one on which the old gentleman was always eloquent. He began his usual rhapsody, but was soon interrupted by a summons to breakfast.

"Who is Mr. Des Ponts?" asked Brydges, when they were seated at table.

"Lawyer by profession, gentleman by practice," said Cade.

"The richest man in Thebes, and the best bred man in Missouri," said Mrs. Marshall.

"He is a French Creole," said the Colonel, "who has the good taste to speak English without lisping. He has good books and good wine, and he buys both himself. The most curious thing about him is that every body owes him money and nobody hates him."

"But," said Clarence, "why does this phoenix of Missourians live in the Theban waste?"

"Ah, that is his most amiable point," said Mrs. Marshall. "He is bound by a promise to the late Madame Des Ponts. She was an enthusiastic Southern woman, who thought a free State the abomination of desolation; even wrote a florid pamphlet called the 'Curse of Canaan'; said she did not see how one could be a Christian and not own slaves, when their means permitted; and I believe honestly doubted whether negroes had souls. She has often said to me that she wished it could be shown that a certain famous text should read in the original, 'Suffer little white children to come unto me.'"

Every one laughed except Mr. Brydges.

"I always thought," the jolly old lady went on, "that Des Ponts recognized as clearly as any one the absurdity of Madame's opinions. But he never disputed with her, and often, when she was hard pressed in a discussion, he would come to her rescue with some brilliant paradox that left one in doubt which side he was really on. She never doubted, I am sure. I never saw a husband so worshiped by his wife. Though one of the proudest of the Shelbys, she delighted in displaying her entire subjection to him. I believe she would have polished his boots if he had permitted it."

"*O si sic omnes*," said the Colonel, and the young men groaned in unison.

Mrs. Marshall continued, scorning the interruption: "She never lost her early infatuation for Des Ponts. The very year she died she and I were in the drawing-room, and Mr. Marshall and he were on the veranda. She looked at him some time in rapt contemplation, and said at last: 'Who could look at that noble form and godlike brow and then think without disgust of Jefferson's claptrap of the equality of men?'"

"She would have preferred," said Cade, "the dictum of our Pomp—'One man is as good as anuddah, an' a heap bettah.'"

"When her last illness came she seemed to regret nothing but leaving Des Ponts. She would not be pacified till he swore—most reluctantly, and after a terrible scene—that he would never take Marie to a Northern State. For she said she hoped still to be with them in spirit, and she could not follow them into Yankee barbarism. So, ever since, poor Des Ponts has lived in that hideous swamp—the Despontine Marshes, as Cade says."

"But why not go South?" said Brydges.

"I imagine he prefers, while keeping his vow faithfully, to live in this extreme corner of slave territory, in sight of free sky and soil."

Brydges bit his lip; and Mrs. Marshall, remembering too late from what latitude he came, talked of pleasant trifles, and put too much sugar in his second cup of coffee by way of apology.

About noon the wagoner, Chris, having reclaimed his cart from its funereal functions, drove up to the back-door, and leaping down, shouldered a vast Saratoga trunk, with which he marched into the house.

"Vere I packs him? Die schoene Fräulein is comin' bimeby a'ready mit 'im Herr Vater. Mein Gott! Die is wunderschoen," he said, grotesquely kissing his stubby finger-ends.

By the time the luggage was bestowed the exiles were at the door.

The Colonel met them with his hearty, old-fashioned courtesy:

"La Rochefoucauld was right. There *is* something in the misfortune of our best friends that does not altogether displease us."

He shook hands with Des Ponts and kissed the neat glove of Marie. She nodded smilingly to the young men, and entered the house with Mrs. Marshall.

"I should have come yesterday," said Des Ponts, "had it not been for that indomitable Shelby pluck of Mimi. We moved the furniture to the second floor in the afternoon; but she still insisted that the river would fall, and so we drank tea in the dismantled parlor, and then sat by the fire till the water poured over the floor and flooded the hearth. 'What am I to do with my feet?' she coolly inquired. 'Would it be quite lady-like to put them on the mantle-piece?' I took her in my arms and waded to the stairs, and carried her up to bed. This morning she got into the skiff from her chamber-window by a rope-ladder—and ever since she calls me Romeo!"

While he was speaking Brydges observed him more closely than he had previously done. He was certainly a strikingly handsome man: a clear, dark skin; black eyes under straight brows; a square forehead and resolute jaw; the mouth almost concealed by a grizzled mustache, a feature not then so common as now; the whole face framed with glossy and luxuriant black curls. There was a strong general resemblance to his daughter; yet they were curiously unlike. The fine animal beauty of his face was in hers lit up and spiritualized by the glancing light of a vivid intelligence. Seeing them together you would think of a head in clay copied in porcelain.

He turned, and his eyes met those of Brydges. Darting a keen glance at the young man, in which one could almost have fancied there was an expression of defiance, he said, abruptly.

"My daughter tells me you are from Mobile. How long have you lived there?"

"All my life."

"Have you relatives of your name in Savannah?"

"No."

Brydges was a little annoyed at this peremptory interrogatory, and so answered very curtly. He did not feel inclined to say that his father had formerly resided in Savannah, but had married and settled in Mobile.

The intense expression vanished at once from the face of Des Ponts. He smiled cheerily, with a flash of splendid white teeth, and said,

"Pardon my summary questions—a relic of my bad lawyer habits. An accidental resemblance, doubtless. Colonel Marshall, Mr. Brydges is a proof of what I have so often told you, that you will find the pure blonde Saxon type oftener in the South than the North."

This remark induced an ethnological controversy between the two gentlemen, which lasted until dinner, and Brydges forgot the explanation he had intended to make.

In the evening Mrs. Marshall said, "Now, Mimi, you must sing for me. I get no music except in these flood times."

"I will sing you something entirely new, by a composer whose name I never heard before—a Mr. Boote, who lives in Florence. A friend of mine traveling in Italy copied and sent it to me. It takes hold of me wonderfully."

She sang in a rich, powerful, vibrating contralto a wild, lawless, but singularly thrilling air, to the words of Kingsley's "Sands o' Dee."

There came over Brydges, as she sang, that sense of mysterious recognition which all have sometimes felt, when every word and gesture falls inevitably into its place, as if we had known and foreseen it all for a thousand years. The other persons in the room became as shadows. He knew the song would cease in a moment, and there would be shadowy words of applause from those outside spectres. But while the wild, sobbing music lasted he and she were alone in the world of sensuous melody. Every touch of her fingers on the pearl and ebony keys fell on his heart, and the song they waked was, "She is mine, and no other's. I love her. I have loved her forever."

The song ended, and the spell was broken. At Cade's request Miss Des Ponts sang that brilliant serenade of Gounod's to Victor Hugo's delicious words, *"Chantez, riez, dormez."* But Brydges only wondered at his ecstasy of a moment before. He looked with critical appreciation at the singer, and saw a superb young girl, as lovely as youth and beauty could make her, singing a showy song in an effective way. But, as if revenging himself for his momentary lapse from self-possession, he thought—"A very pretty girl—a little too *prononcée*—not infrequently slangy—needs a year or two of better society than she can find in Thebes."

The next day Miss Des Ponts started for a gallop on the Carthage road, attended by her two cavaliers. Cade deserted very soon, riding off to visit the Colonel's farm, north of the town. "It is a remarkably porous soil," said Cade. "Absorbs every thing you put on it, and leaves no trace. Mimi, I hold you responsible for Mr. Brydges."

They rode an hour or two through the thick timber and the sunny lanes, and returned excellent friends. There was no resisting the charm of Marie's directness and sincerity. Her character had something manly in its frank, fearless honesty.

He was surprised at her unaffected sense of her own shortcomings. "I suspect it is not best for me to live as I do. Mamma died when I was a child, and I have grown up lawlessly with Victor. There—a new impropriety! I have always called him by his first name; instead of correcting me, he laughed and kissed me. So when I talked slang, till I am afraid I sometimes trip that way now, when I am old enough to know better. I read his books and his newspapers, and had no other education until Mrs. Marshall positively dragooned him into letting me go to school. I staid two years at the Visitation in St. Louis, and learned some music; then ran away and came back to him, and found him, I am sure, ten years older by the separation. I will not leave him again. And yet I know we ought not to live in that *triste* little town. I have so often begged him to go South, or to Congress, or somewhere. With his great talents and influence he could do every thing in politics. But he detests the very name. I believe he cares for nothing but me."

These words were uttered with an intonation indescribably sweet and winning. The great brown eyes were softened with unshed tears. But before Brydges could speak she struck her horse a smart blow with the riding-whip, and they went dashing homeward, accompanied by a cloud of dust and the yelping of scandalized curs.

The days passed on pleasantly enough with walking and riding and making visits in Moscow, where Marie knew every body and was universally admired. Mr. Des Ponts went every morning to Thebes, and passed an hour or two in his skiff, going from window to window of those acquaintances who valorously remained in their upper rooms, lulled nightly to sleep by the rushing of waters under their floors. Day after day Mr. Brydges said, resolutely, "I go to-morrow." But the weather was finer than he had ever seen, the skies bluer than ever had shone, and the Marshalls were the pleasantest hosts he ever had met. So he lingered, and still was traveling always into the borders of the Enchanted Land, which is as old as nature, yet newer and fresher and stranger than any thing on earth, to each young heart that finds it. He never asked himself how far he should go. The path was smooth and enticing, the air subtle and fine. Continually just beyond there was a bank of rare blossoms, a splendor of sunlight on the emerald lawns. He would go that far, and then? All the while the shuttle of Fate was flying swiftly about him, and weaving into the web of his life a richness and brilliancy it had never known.

One evening he and Miss Des Fonts were sitting alone on the veranda. They had been talking for an hour. The conversation was of the river, of the news, of books; at first animated, then languid, till it dropped into an embarrassed silence. Clarence had given himself utterly up to the delight of his eyes. Her delicate profile was defined against the clear dark sky of the west. The light of the young May moon lay on her rippled hair. She seemed in the faint glimmer almost too lovely to be real. As the young man gazed at her he forgot that she was talking, and even answered her questions at random. Surprised and perplexed, she ceased speaking.

He sat facing the river and the west, where the silver crescent hung above the Missouri hills. Forced by her silence to say something, he said, hastily, "Turn to the left and look at the new moon. It will bring you great good luck this month."

He seemed to himself to speak involuntarily—he listened with interest to his own words.

She turned to him. "I will not look at the moon. I want no luck. I am happy enough. Besides," she added, with a smile as delicate as the starlight, "I can see the moon now, in your eyes."

"Can you see any thing else there?"

She turned away, her heart beating with a vague apprehension.

"Can you see that I love you? that I worship you? that my free-will is gone? that—I love you?"

She covered her face with her hands.

"I have been living here in a dream. I see now what it means. It is fatal for good or ill. My whole life fails if I go from here without you. Marie, will you go with me?"

He paused for a moment.

"If you say nothing I shall go mad with a false hope."

She turned her glowing face toward him. Even in that dim light the radiance of a new and wonderful happiness shone in her perfect features with a faint opaline gleam. But her manner was more quiet and self-possessed than usual as she said,

"I wish you would bring my father to me."

"But, Miss Des Ponts, shall I not have one word—?"

"Please bring my father," she insisted, in a low, appealing tone that there was no resisting.

When they came out she went to her father and leaned upon his arm. In spite of his intense anxiety Brydges could not but admire the statuesque beauty of the group. So Iphigenia must have clung at Aulis to the King of Men; and so the greatest of the Greeks must have folded in his strong arm the most beautiful, protecting her against all the world but him.

"Victor, Mr. Brydges has asked me to be his wife. I will not answer without your sanction."

"My darling, follow your heart, and you will make me only less happy than yourself."

She gave Clarence her hand and said, "I never dreamed I could love two beings as I love my father and you."

Des Ponts went in, with a strange contest of pleasure and pain in his heart, and left the lovers in the dim light of the setting moon.

Before Clarence slept he wrote a long letter to his father, announcing his engagement and giving many details of the character and position of the Des Ponts. He did not ask his father's consent formally. He was so thoroughly convinced of the propriety of his action that he would have disregarded his father's absolute veto. But, nevertheless, he awaited with some interest Mr. Brydges's reply.

Among the occasional visitors at Fort Johnstone was a friend of Mr. Marshall, a lawyer of Moscow, with whose graceful, though somewhat formal bearing, measured speech, and thorough moderation, as well in speech as in opinion, Clarence was much impressed. One night when this gentleman was gone Mrs. Marshall said, "You would scarcely suppose that Mr. X_____ had been tried for murder and acquitted by a quibble?"

Brydges expressed his surprise.

"He was one of the slayers of the Mormon prophet Joe Smith, at our county jail."

"By-the-way, Clarence," said Cade, "would you not like to drive out to-morrow and see where the Church seed was spilled?"

Brydges gladly assented; and the young men drove over the prairie in the cool of the morning. After visiting the scene of the tragedy, Clarence, who had been remarkably taciturn and thoughtful all the morning, said, abruptly,

"I wish you would present me to your County Clerk. I want a marriage license."

"Bravo!" shouted Cade. "I see you never want to come here again. But it is not necessary. I can get your license whenever you want it."

"I may want it very soon. You know, Cade, I am fixed upon this marriage. No opposition from my father could change me. But Des Ponts and Marie are very spirited people. If my father should be whimsical enough to object, they might take umbrage. But if I could be married at once and go home with Marie, Monsieur *mon père* would yield to her beauty and grace as readily as did Monsieur his son."

"You are Sam Slick and Machiavel rolled into one. Here we are at the court-house."

They got the license and drove home.

"Do you think they will consent to this chain-lightning plan of yours?"

"I do not think Marie will require much time. I imagine that in Thebes she has been uncorrupted by the mania of shopping. I *am* a little afraid of Des Ponts."

But to his surprise Des Ponts assented with alacrity to an immediate marriage. He said he should soon be compelled to make a journey to the East—perhaps to Europe. He would be glad to see his daughter's happiness secured before he started.

Marie at first protested loudly, but finding no sympathy in her lover or her father she flew to Mrs. Marshall, but found her equally hard-hearted.

"Nonsense, child," said the merry old lady. "We can make you lovely in half an hour. Why, Marshall proposed to me in this very fort while the long-roll was beating one evening, and we were married before the guard was out."

Marie yielded with a pretty girlish grace, that had come in these last days as the finishing charm of a character formerly, perhaps, too firm and self-reliant. Des Ponts's restlessness and anxiety seemed to increase hour by hour. He spent much of his time in Thebes arranging his papers and closing up pending affairs. The flood had now subsided, and a half-drowned slimy life began to move sluggishly through the soft black streets. He alleged to every one urgent business as an excuse for his sudden and unwonted activity. He did not say distinctly where he was going, but spoke sometimes of New Orleans, and oftener of Europe.

"Why will you not go with us?" asked Clarence.

"Later I hope to join you," he would answer, with a smile heart-breaking in the sadness that tried to be gay.

The trunks were packed and sent to the wharf. The bride stood on the veranda dressed for travel, as bright in her blushes and tears as a morning of April. Good Mrs. Marshall, quite melted by her sympathetic happiness, was laughing and crying together, and giving Marie a world of motherly last words.

A red-faced, sleepy-eyed youth came up and asked for Mr. Brydges. "Here's a tallygraft fur him."

Clarence opened the envelope hastily and said, "How unfortunate! Father has started to come to the wedding, and is at St. Louis—says he will leave on this evening's packet. I must send him a telegram to wait there for us."

He wrote the dispatch, and was about handing it to the shabby messenger when Colonel Marshall said, "I will send it to the office by Thomas. I don't think this beery youth is quite awake yet."

"I regret, Mr. Des Ponts," said Clarence, "that you are not to meet my father here. You may be acquaintances, after all. My father lived in Savannah some thirty years ago."

At this moment the steamer rounded the point to the north, and her shrill whistle broke off the conversation. Des Ponts turned ashy pale. His daughter clung to him one instant. There was a confusion of hurried farewells, and the young people drove away to the wharf. In the slanting sunshine of the early morning the clouds of dust raised by their carriage-wheels turned to a rosy halo in which they passed out of sight.

There was a moment of silence. It was broken by Des Ponts, who said, in a husky voice, "Good-by, my old friends. I shall not attempt to thank you enough for your life-long goodness to me and mine."

He took a packet from his paletot and handed it to Colonel Marshall. "This contains my will and one or two other trifles. I am going away for a while—"

"But not immediately?"

"Yes. I can finish to-day the little matters that remain in Thebes. I want to—' He paused, as if in doubt; then continued, in a manner strangely different from his usual one, "I have been tormented all night by impish dreams; and this morning I feel all abroad. I was always rather a lazy man, but the prospect of an absolute *far niente* is by no means alluring. My work in life is done—" Seeing the look of distress on the face of his friends, he forced a smile and said, "Perhaps I shall learn to enjoy the play-time."

"Yes, we will talk that over at tea," said Mrs. Marshall. "You must certainly stay with us now till your departure."

"Well, well, I will come back to-night."

Then, as he was going to the door, he turned and said, "Colonel, it has been a quarter of a century since I heard Booth, yet all this morning I have been haunted by his tones in the words: 'Thou wouldst not think how ill all's here about my heart.' And the other phrase: 'If it be now, 'tis not to come; if it be not to come, it will be now; *if it be not now, yet it will come.*'"

That afternoon Cade Marshall picked up in the library the telegram which Brydges had dropped, and exclaimed,

"Here's a contretemps! This telegram arrived yesterday. That tipsy rascal forgot to deliver it."

"That *is* awkward," said the Colonel. "We can do nothing now but go to the landing for Mr. Brydges and explain the mistake. It is not so bad, after all. He can meet Des Ponts here, and will be sure to like him. Marie and Clarence can pass a day or two pleasantly in St. Louis.

Des Ponts did not return to tea. The steamer was late in coming. All the afternoon the Marshalls watched for it. It was already dark when the Colonel saw the red head-lights shining far down the river. Even while he looked he saw, to his horror, a bright tongue of flame darting from the lower deck and rapidly climbing up the side. It seemed but a moment until the steamer was wrapped in a lurid blaze that blotted out the moonlight and gleamed balefully over the low bottoms to the distant bluffs.

Des Ponts saw it also, midway of the river. He had been detained in Thebes until he was too late for the ferry, and had taken his skiff to row across in the cool fresh night. The fine air and the exercise of rowing kindled his blood, and he threw off the depression that had weighed upon him during the day. Resting on his oars a moment and looking about him, he saw the steamer coming around the bar, and in an instant observed the red jet of fire that spurted from the engine-deck. He turned and rowed to the spot as fast as his strong arms and the swift current could carry him, but before he was there the doomed vessel, all pine and paint and tinder, a most delicate morsel for the fire-fiend, was enveloped in a shroud of flame. The water was filled with struggling and drowning passengers. One of these Des Ponts seized, and, in doing so, dropped an oar. By the time he had lifted the exhausted man into the skiff they had drifted some distance astern of the blazing wreck. Perceiving he had lost an oar, he stood in the stern of his boat to scull back to where others were still struggling. The glare of the conflagration was full in his face. His hat had fallen, and his fine head was brilliantly relieved against the dark like a portrait of Rembrandt.

The man he had saved, lying in the bow, burst into a loud laugh.

Des Ponts felt the blood freezing in his veins. A shudder passed over his frame so powerful that the boat trembled with it. The horror that had tagged him through life was there, open-mouthed, in his path. But he still held his oar with a grip of iron, and stood as motionless as marble.

"Sam, you're a d____d lucky nigger! You have saved your hide forty by picking me up to-night."

Des Ponts trembled again, with the ghost of the old slavish terror that stirred in his soul. He remembered, with horrible humiliation, the story of Herodotus, where the Scythians quelled a triumphant army of slaves by dropping their swords and attacking with their riding-whips. He felt in every fibre of his being that the story was true.

"Come, come, Sam, don't be sulky," said the man in the bow, with a tone meant to be good-natured. "Row me ashore, and leave those rats to swim for it. I sha'n't be hard on you if you behave yourself. How is Clarence?"

"Your son has married my daughter," said Des Ponts.

"Capital!" laughed Brydges. "The girl will come along without any row."

These brutal words recalled Des Ponts to himself. A light which was almost triumph came into his eyes.

"Victor Brydges," he said, firmly and quietly, "I do not wish to play at comedy with you. I am your boy Sam. I have no legal existence, you say; I have no child, no name. Granting this, your son is legally married to the natural daughter of Miss Julia Shelby of Glenarthur."

Brydges saw that this calm statement was incontrovertible. In his sullen rage he fumbled in his waistband, and drawing a dirk, sprang at Des Ponts and struck him in the face. Des Ponts seized and disarmed him, throwing him back heavily into the bow. He tossed the dirk, wet with his own blood, into the river.

"You see how strong I am, and how weak you are, Victor Brydges. If you come at me again I will kill you."

In the slight scuffle he had regained his self-possession. He seated himself on one of the thwarts, facing Brydges. The boat floated with the current. They were nearly out of the glare of the burning boat, but there was light enough to show the firm-set face of Des Ponts, where the streaming blood drew lines of crimson across its ghastly pallor. There was no fear in it now, only the paleness of cool and self-conscious desperation.

"In fifteen minutes," he said, "this current will carry us ashore on Fox Island. We must settle our differences in that time. Unless you come to my terms you shall never leave this boat alive."

"Let's hear your terms," said Brydges.

"Our children are married and happy. Let them alone. I have given my daughter a dowry of one hundred thousand dollars. I will give you the highest market-price for myself. In return, you will bind yourself by oath, in writing, to silence—that is all."

"Sam! I will be candid with you. I think you are lying. You have not so much money. If you have, it is mine already. Consent to break up this marriage, pay me for yourself and the girl, and we will fix it up without scandal. I don't forget we are foster-brothers. You have received much kindness from my family—"

"Stop there! I was brought up with you to serve you. I learned French to be useful to you when you went abroad. I studied at the University to coach you through. I got my degree, and you failed. When at last I offered to buy myself and remain in France, you cursed me and struck me; and after that you were fool enough to trust me. You made me use my credit at the Prefecture of Police to get you a passport under the name of Des Ponts, to assist you in some scandalous intrigue. I swear that until I had that passport in my hands I never dreamed of running away."

"It has played the devil with you at last. I should never have found you but for that name in Clarence's letter."

"I met and married my wife under that name. I had made it honorable, and could not change it."

"Well, what do you say to my terms?"

"Victor Brydges," said Des Ponts, with solemn earnestness, "our children are married and happy. I am ready to die for the good of my daughter, and you must die for the good of your son, unless you accept my offer."

While he spoke Brydges was looking about him. He saw the boat had drifted so near to the low, willowy island that he could easily swim that distance. He felt himself unequal to another grapple with Des Ponts. His whole soul revolted against making any compromise with his slave. He slid over the boat's side with the quickness of an otter. Des Ponts started to his feet. "God have mercy on us both!" he murmured, hoarsely. As the head of Brydges came to the surface he plunged into the rapid current, and the foster-brothers went to the bottom locked in each other's arms.

They were found in the same posture two days later, lying on the shining sand. The Marshalls mourned and buried them side by side. Mrs. Marshall concluded a long and tender letter to Marie with these words:

"My dear children, from their graves your beloved fathers —one of whom lost his precious life in this noble effort to rescue the other from the waves—exhort you continually to love one another."

Red, White, and Blue (1861)

It was the 15th of April, 1861—a day to be recorded—to be remembered; for on this day, across countless wires, flashed the startling intelligence, "SURRENDER OF THE FORT AND GARRISON!   75,000 MILITIA CALLED FOR!"

Just back from Europe, in the midst of the rose odors of a lady's boudoir, and surrounded by the costly preparations for a party—laces and jewels and flowers—Edgar Mayne was reading this; Edgar Mayne—sound of heart as of limb—a young Hercules, ardent and impetuous, who for the last three years, at English clubs, and French salons, and Roman cafés, had raved and roared his patriotic belief in the Government of these United States with true American zeal. And now drums were beating and bugles blowing at its dissolution.

"75,000 men! Do you hear that, Caroline? I tell you before three months have elapsed we shall be occupied in fighting, and not flirting; so you might as well put up your flowers and flounces, and all this gauze folly," settling a strong hand down with a contemptuous crush on flowers, and flounces, and "folly."

"75,000! Do you realize it, Caroline?" looking with large brown eyes over the newspaper at the girl there, decking a gauze gown with slips of scarlet kalmia and beads of golden grain. She tossed her head at him with an air.

"Bah! blonde and flowers—that's all the women of to-day are fit for! You girls! what do you care for your country, for liberty or tyranny, so that you can have your fineries?" and rising, he half smiled at his own earnestness, and, passing her, let the strong hand drop caressingly upon her loose silky hair, dropping a remark with it to soften his previous brusquerie; for Edgar Mayne was too well bred to be deliberately rude, *even to his own sister*.

Later in the day, as he sat by the fire absorbed in an evening journal, the mistress of the boudoir put her gem-like face between him and the news with a question:

"Will the state of the country allow you to accompany me to Mrs. Welles's to-night, Edgar?"

He pinched the vivid cheek, and with a little grimace made answer,

"You are pretty, Carrie; but such a doll!" Then he goes railing off, as young men like to do, "Oh you women, you pretty women, Carrie."

'To think men can not take you, sweet,
And enfold you,
Ay and hold you,
And so keep you, what they make you, sweet!'

Singing the German waltz, she went up the stairs. Three hours after she came down trilling the bars of a Redowa, and enveloped in a white mist of drapery, blooming with flowers—the scarlet kalmia and beads of yellow grain nodding in her hair of dense black—hair cloudy and soft beside a face of dappled rose and white, and violet eyes hiding darkly underneath darker brows and heavy fringes.

Through the mystic changes of the German waltz, and the sweet sliding cadences of the Redowa, there went weaving a solemn strain of dissonance. Into the pauses of the dance stole subtle languors—flowers faded, banners drooped, and the wind flung in through opened windows a quivering, shuddering sigh which every heart repeated.

"How stupid every thing seems! What is the matter?—what ails the night?" asked Caroline Mayne of her companion, young Ryversant, in a disappointed, petulant tone.

He pushed a curtain aside, and they stood in the conservatory.

"What ails the night, Miss Caroline? We've had a shock—an electric shock—and we are a little stunned by it. One can't help thinking, while the horns and bugles are playing in there, of how they will sound a month hence, perhaps, when the bullets are whizzing round our heads."

"Do you really think it will come to that, Mr. Ryversant?"

"I think it is already here."

"Yes, I know there has been a call for troops; but I fancied there'd be a bluster, and then—"

"And then what, Miss Caroline?"

"Why, that both parties would keep on the defensive a while, but that it would finally be settled without bloodshed."

"It will be settled only with the shedding of the best and bravest blood in the country."

She mused. At length, speaking half absently: "I wonder who will go?"

"I shall go, Miss Caroline."

"You!"—a little start of surprise, covered by a laugh of incredulity; then an exclamation, as she held out a hand with its snowy glove spotted and streaked with crimson stains.

"What is it? Ah! I see; you have cut your hand on that vile Egyptian urn against which you leaned. I did once in this very spot"; and he took the hand commiseratingly.

"No, no, it is nothing of the kind; it is only the red orchis that you gave me—I crushed it between my fingers."

There was a glow upon her cheek as fiery as the red orchis's stain, and a stormy gloom gathering in her eyes, while the little stained palm was dented and crushed by the fingers yet trembling from the effort.

"Ugh! how it looks like blood!" she went on. "Yes, take it off—do. I hope it isn't an omen." "An omen?"

"Yes, of real bloodshed, and of what may follow if what you say comes true—of death, you know."

"Ah!" and a lifted look of lofty pain crossed his face. "The sin is great, but it shall be washed away in a nation's blood!"

The rapt expression was yet in his eyes as the little hand, soft and cold, lay uncovered in his own; and the absent air with which he kissed it could no woman with a heart and soul gainsay. But the cool touch of the slight fingers brought him back—he was but a man, and a young and ardent one. Lingering over the fair, little hand, he said, "I want a keepsake to take away with me when I go, Miss Caroline—a guerdon of emprise. Give me this little glove, with its mock blood-stains. It is a fitting token of the present—a symbol of the 'blood-red blossom of war.'"

She shuddered visibly. "Oh no, no, Mr. Ryversant, not that!"

The sudden passion of her manner, the gathering color, the kindling eyes! Up sprang the hope that for six months had been living and dying in his heart. In a moment all the conventionalities had swept by."

"But you will give me something! Oh, Caroline, give me yourself!" And the young fellow bent down his head, and hid his eyes against the little soft hand in that moment of suspense.

There came a stir—a lifted curtain drenched the moonlight in a flood of gas. A ripple of laughter, a rustle of silk, and the apartment had two other occupants. One, a woman, had quickly caught the spirit of the scene. And this woman? She hated Caroline Mayne as women hate sometimes from sheer antagonism of youth and beauty; and hating her, she know her weak points. She knew that Caroline Mayne had the dangerous reputation of a Clare Vere de Vere—whether deserved or no she did not care to inquire. So, with one of those mischievous impulses which tempt some souls, she dropped this small sneer at their feet.

"Oh! just in time to interrupt your rejection, Mr. Ryversant."

And Caroline Mayne— what did she do? A splendid thing. One moment she hesitated, while the fiery flame of wounded delicacy rose to her cheek and kindled in her eyes. Then, quite clearly, though a little haughty of tone, and with an inscrutable depth in her glance, she made answer: "You are just in time to give me your congratulations, Miss Wyld. I am happy in owing allegiance to Mr. Ryversant." And over Mr. Ryversant's arm a little ungloved hand went stealing.

If ten minutes before he had thought Caroline Mayne the dearest and fairest of women, what did he think now, in view of her charming courage, her proud and tender generosity? In view of it, his heart thrilling with its sudden rapture of acceptance, a new feeling of reverence touched him so deeply that eyes filled and cheeks flushed. "If I am ever tempted," he said unto himself, "to judge this woman in anger, the memory of this night shall soften all later memories."

Into the German waltz no longer wound the solemn

strains of dissonance. The wind no longer sighed in fitful melancholy, the flowers no longer drooped; Death's head had vanished from the feast, and the eternal flower of love bloomed in its place. Riding home, Edgar Mayne asked his sister,

"What did Lou Wyld mean by your being a subject for congratulation? She met me as she went to her carriage, and said she had just congratulated you on your engagement. Some of her nonsense, I suppose."

"No, it was quite true"; and Caroline, as briefly as possible, related the circumstances of the last half hour. Brief as the relation was, Edgar Mayne perceived in those "circumstances" the peculiar nobility which had so touched the soul of Jerome Ryversant. He bent forward, and scanned her face—touched the lovely falling hair, and the drooping kalmia, and the "gauze folly."

"Carrie, I didn't think it was in you."

"To love?"

"To be so brave. Carrie, do you know what you have done? By this one act you have bound Jerome Ryversant to you by a bond of tender admiration which years of ordinary devotion would not have accomplished."

"You overrate it. I don't see."

"You little girl!" coming over, unchecked now by the clouds of "gauze folly," to sit beside her and put his arm about her. "Don't you see that you did it for him. I see, and so did he, that your soul rose to meet the occasion because you were assailed in your pride and tenderness for him. It wasn't an easy thing to do, Carrie. I can fancy the color mounting, and the storm in your eyes; but it was easier than to let the shadow of a momentary mortification or pain rest upon your lover. No, I didn't think it was in you, Carrie. I give you my congratulations"; bending forward and touching his lips to hers.

"She is really quite splendid!" he thought. "I am glad I know her better."

Did he know her better? Did she know herself better? Let us see.

Three days followed of congratulation, of happiness. The pretty boudoir was odorous with the rarest flowers that a lover could find, and redolent with the fair presences of youth and beauty. Every hour he thought— this young lover— "She is the noblest woman in the world!"

Outside this rose-Eden of youth, and beauty, and happiness the three days were set to sadder music while the 75,000 loyal souls were rapidly gathering under the Stars and Stripes. Did Jerome Ryversant forget that he had promised himself to his country in this newer and nearer promise? In the fair fetters of this rose-Eden did he forget his allegiance to his native land? He was only waiting. At the close of the three days there would be time enough for parting words. So the three days went in a trance of happiness. He saw the sun set upon the last with a sigh that was like the echo of a farewell; and with the sigh yet upon his lips he sought her presence. She was standing by the window, the warm mellow light bathing her beauty in a celestial bloom. The lovely hair half falling, as he liked it best—the lovely figure wearing the colors he approved—and on her breast and in her hair the very flowers he had given her in the morning. The pang of parting struck deeper. She came forward in her pretty, stately way, her head drooped to him, her proud lips melting into a smile, and a conscious color rising.

"What is the matter? Has any body hurt you? as we say to little Nell," she asked him. He never answered; but the glance he dropped down upon her, yearning and mournful, the touch of his hand, lingering and tender, like a benediction upon her head, while a sigh tore up from his heart like a sob—all this was more eloquent than words, and in affright she put her question a second time with affectionate alarm.

"What *is* the matter, dear? What has happened?"

He drew her nearer, bending down his gaze to meet hers.

"I was thinking of what *is* to happen, dearest—that the time draws nearer. It seems harder now, though I have the heart I sought for a 'guerdon of emprise.'"

She looked puzzled, shook her head, and said, questioningly, "I don't understand."

He watched her a moment as she leaned against his arm—soft tints of rose, and violet darks—all a flower made to wear in one's bosom, to

"Sing and say for,
Watch and pray for."

And as he watched a fear shot into his heart—she didn't understand! Then he said, softly, drawing her closer still, to ease the ache.

"My regiment you know, it leaves soon."

"Well?"

Wouldn't she understand?

He waited a second—her face was out of sight—he was: holding it in his breast; and she was quite still. Presently he spoke,

"I go with it as—"

"You!" The utter coldness of the tone, the ringing resonance, as she ejaculated this one word, sounded like an accusation—like an accusation, pale and fierce, rose the clear-cut face, and she looked at him. He met the gaze tenderly, but sorrowfully. She waited for him to speak.

"You have forgotten, dear," he said at length, "that"—

he paused a moment, hushing his heart at the memory of "that time"—"you have forgotten I told you four nights ago that I was going."

"Then—but now—all is changed since then. Is life no dearer to you? Do you owe it to none other than yourself?" The clear-cut face gathered color, and the eyes began to fill with hot tears.

"Caroline!"—he met the angry crimson, the tearful tones, with a firm gaze: he answered steadily, "I owe it to my country!"

She laughed in bitter scorn, then said, derisively, "To your country! Wait till you are needed more imperatively; thousands are ready to go, are going; thousands abler than you. Why should you rush thus hastily forward? It is a madness; a piece of folly: you are excited with the occasion. Because others are going you go; and you call it patriotism, courage. It is neither; you are a coward, because you dare not stay behind. And more than that, you love your own glory better than you love me!"

Conflicting passions reflected themselves in the face of her listener. Sorrow, tenderness, and a man's honor shone there: all three dictated his reply:

"Caroline, you do not know what you say, or you would never say it. I love you, because I honor you and admire you above all other women. I love you as I love all that is beautiful and true; for you are to me the representative of every thing beautiful and true: and so to love you is to love my honor and duty. How then could I do less?"

The passionate tears she shed, the wild words of denial she uttered, were not all passion and wildness. It was her first grief; and out of an aching heart sprang all this fierce emotion. From the soul's most sacred recesses of tenderness came the hot tide of agony that translated itself in taunts and reproaches. Perhaps something of this was apparent to her listener; for through the harshest taunt, the cruelest reproach, he possessed himself. Perhaps one memory still more possessed him—a remembrance of that night, four days agone, when the world was transfigured for him, and when on the altar of his soul he made a vow to let all judgments soften to that hour. They softened now into clear, concise answers, perfectly manly, and perfectly tender; but they failed to convince or soften. To all this forbearance she returned only sharp reproach or bitter scorn, and lastly drew from her finger its one special ring, dropped it into his hand, from whence it fell untaken to the floor, gave him her stateliest courtesy for a "good-by," and swept from the room. Half stupefied with the shock, the young fellow stood a moment gazing vacantly before him, murmuring, incoherently, "And this is the end—this is the end!"

It was thus Edgar Mayne found him. He went up to him asking the same question his sister had put a few minutes before under such different circumstances, "What is the matter?" but in that instant his eye caught the gleam of the diamond flashing out like a star against the soft glooms of the carpet. "Ah!" and he looked sadly into the face before him, as he lifted it—"A lover's quarrel!" A bad time for that now, on the eve of his departure, however. He would ask no questions; but all questions were anticipated, were answered in a few brief words.

Edgar Mayne was indignant.

"The girl is crazy!" he ejaculated, and was rushing from the rooms to tell her so, to bring her down before them, in his impulse, when the calmer reason of Jerome Ryversant stayed him. But after, when he had bade his guest good-night, with tears in his eyes, and haunted by his suffering face, he sought her. He was not prepared for the pale look of agony that met him, and his greeting softened; but his errand was enough to rouse her, and something of the old scorn returned to her.

"But you can not see," he returned, impatiently, to her persistent accusations, "that he had pledged not only his word, but his heart and soul, to this cause in the very outset."

"That was before!—that was before!" she exclaimed, with quick significance; "and after, when hundreds are pressing forward, and many rejected, why should he leave me, and so soon? No, do not argue with me—I am only secondary. I thought him finer than other men, but I was mistaken; it is their own glory first—then a woman's love. If I never marry I will not take a man who makes me second in his heart. I must reign there, the first consideration; his first honor and glory, as he shall reign in mine."

"But—" He stopped, wise enough to see that only time could open her eyes to her error—time and remorse; that his words were wasted; and worse than that, adding still more to her determination.

As abruptly as he had entered he left her presence, left her to the sharp, burning pain, the consuming passion, that devastates such proud, concentrative natures.

Thus days went on in this wild inward war which gave no outward sign. In the time she asked no questions, she made no allusion to the past; but secretly and alone she devoured every crumb of information that the newspapers offered. She, who hated politics and newspapers!

One day, in a long list of names, she read one that

sent every vestige of color from her cheek—Jerome Ryversant! If she had had any hope of his relenting, it was over now; but even here she gave no sign—there was still an outward calm.

Three days more and he would be gone. Gone! it was a bitter word.

The night of the third day came drearily to many a heart—to none more drearily than to her, sitting apart and alone in a rose-hued boudoir. The sickly scent of faded flowers filled the room—his flowers. The curtains were undrawn, the chairs and couches still strewn with the trifles that had occupied them ten days agone. All as *he* had left it. In this sepulchre the proud heart straggled on.

For these last three days her brother had caught no glimpse of her. But on the last night, somewhere between the hours of twelve and one, a little knock came outside his door, and her voice called him. He was sitting writing, and, somewhat startled, bade her come in. The face that greeted him startled still more. Its rose-bloom was gone—youth itself seemed to have departed. So touching was the sight that his eyes filled, and he received her with more kindliness than he had evinced since that fatal night. Was she ill? he inquired.

She hesitated a moment, then told her errand. She would see Jerome Ryversant once more before he sailed. Would her brother aid her to this? There was no time to lose, for at dawn they might have left the city; but let him understand her: she had not changed her mind—this was not to acknowledge that —it was no reunion, but *she would see him once again!*

At what he considered unpardonable obstinacy, Edgar Mayne was again indignant; but another look at the pale, worn face, and he consented to undertake the mission.

To Jerome Ryversant he communicated the letter and spirit of her words. For a moment his eye blazed, and the man's passion rose angrily. Then the memory of another night came up. He remembered her, proud and tender and brave for his sake; he remembered his vow as well, and signified his readiness to go to her.

The lights were all down but one in the "rose-Eden"— that one, burning through pale purple glass, sent forth over the room a mystical radiance. Into this room Edgar Mayne conducted young Ryversant, leaving him at the door.

As the two looked at each other after the door closed upon them, they realized, perhaps, something more of the change suffering had wrought. But to her it had wrought much more of change in these three days than the whole time had wrought to him. He was upheld by the sublime knowledge of sacrifice, of patriotism, of right; plunged, too, into the midst of unparalleled excitements.

She, nursing an insane sense of wrong, born of her defective education as a woman—of her ignorance; alone, too, in the inaction of domestic life, had hung out the pale colors of distress. Seeing her thus, he knew she loved him, though still blinded to the right. Seeing *him*, with a flush upon his cheek, uniformed and eager, she still less believed his love.

So her voice came coldly:

"I sent for you," she said, slowly, and with painful effort. "We parted angrily, which was not wise nor well for what may be a final parting. In my view of your undertaking I yet hold the same opinions; but we will part as friends should."

He came forward and took her hands. Once more he pleaded with her. She heard him sadly, not angrily, but yet unbelieving. He glanced down upon the fair little hands he held, but his ring had never been replaced. She was fearfully in earnest then—it was only a friendly "good-by." So, bending down, he dropped a kiss upon the two hands; and lifting his head, with a "God bless you, Caroline!" was about to go, when the ghastly pallor of her face, the faint drooping of her figure, stayed him. She had no strength, nor any will to resist, as he took her in his arms. Very quietly she rested there, and when once or twice his hand went caressingly down her hair a tear forced itself through the shut eyelids.

At length, rousing herself, with a motion of her hand she bent his head and voluntarily hissed him, "Good-by!" He held her tightly a moment more—then the rose boudoir had but one occupant, and this one was heedless of all pain and passion until the dawn recalled her from her unconsciousness to life and misery.

Later, her maid coming in opened the window, and the fresh draught blowing through fluttered something that looked like a star-flower from its resting-place upon the floor, and blew it to her breast. She shuddered; then kissed it passionately—one of those little silken emblems—a cockade of red, white, and blue. Last night it glittered on the breast of Jerome Ryversant. Almost at the very instant a boy's young voice ascended, lark-like, singing,

"With her flag proudly floating before her,
The boast of the red, white, and blue!"

Following this wound the notes of a bugle; then the long-rolling call of a drum; and the city was astir with the warlike preparations.

How that morning went she never knew, and other mornings came finding her saddened but alert, with a serious watchfulness. A week after, when her brother announced his own determination to join in the struggle, she did not gainsay it.

On her table now, in place of romances, newspapers and books pertaining to the various struggles for liberty in other countries, and all manner of patriotic addresses that had gone forth from this, found place. She was learning a new lesson. It filled her soul with sorrow and perplexity, but it elevated and enlarged it.

So the days lengthened into weeks.

There came at last a day that will never be forgotten. In one portion of the land church bells were ringing and organ strains ascending on the summer air. In another,

"All into the valley of Death
Rode the six hundred."

Sitting in church that morning, through the solemn sweetness of the chants Caroline Mayne was haunted by one sentence—"I owe it to my country!" The organ strains sounded to her like the dirge of hope, and the hymn had notes of wailing in it. "I owe it to my country!" That noble life! Was he even then, perhaps, giving it up? She drooped her flushed face, lifting her handkerchief as a shield, when lo! there dropped from out its folds the little silken token he had left behind—red, white, and blue! At such times, to imaginative persons, such simple occurrences come like omens. As such it came to her; and there, in the summer warmth, she grew chill with her emotions.

When, shortly afterward, the awful news came of that vain struggle she felt that her soul had been warned. Then followed the uncertainty of life or death for the beloved. In silence and alone she waited.

One day the bells rang, the cannon roared, and shouts of welcome rent the air. At a sheltered window a fair figure stoled in white watched the returning heroes.

Her watch is rewarded: but she can scarcely see for tears as a proud head lifts itself above the others to her vision; and in close company her brother—Edgar Mayne—both safe and before her!

When a bouquet, small and delicate, fell at Jerome Ryversant's feet, he did not doubt its source nor its meaning as he looked at it. A bunch of scarlet kalmias, and red orchis, and beads of golden grain surrounding one rose—a white rose, the heart's gift—and girdling it all a circle of laurel. Thus she spoke to him from her sheltered window. Thus she made her confessions.

Later, when he held her to his heart, with the same noble simplicity which had so endeared her at first, she briefly said,

"I was wrong, and you were right; but I sinned through ignorance. Life has wider meanings to me now. This war has been my education."

How truly she said he began to realize as he saw with what clear perceptions she put mere personal ends away and flung her sympathies into the common cause. He realized it more fully when, a month later, sitting in the "rose-Eden," he put his future in her hands. Should he stay or go? A little lower dropped the head, a little colder grew the clasping hand, a little broken came the sweetest voice, as she answered:

"If three months ago the country needed the services of brave men, we know it needs them now. As you would give up for its cause what is dearer than your own life, I give what is dearer than mine."

While we await the result of this war to our country let us hope that its lessons have been thus nobly received, and that from the claims of pleasure, the fetters of fashion, other women may be able to renounce mere personal ends, and give up with such spiritual insight of love what is dearer than their own lives—what is dearer than any life— a country's salvation. And when they drape their rooms with banners and silken symbols, let them think of the meaning of this—"Red, White, and Blue."

APPENDIX

The Minstrel: A Tale of Normandy

And they are gone. Ay, ages long ago
These lovers fled away into the storm.

Keats

The dusk of a November evening was gathering around the castle of Mermaison. The sun had sunk in fiery haze, and a thick white mist was creeping slowly up from the Northern sea. The solemn hush in the air betokened an approaching storm and its earliest notes of onset were sounded in the swinging boughs of the oaks and in the creaking of the whirling vanes. The rooks were wending their noisy flight to their nests and in the distance the weary serfs with uncouth oaths and angry shouts were urging homeward their reluctant herds. The night was coming on with the rapidity of Autumn. A gloomy grandeur was imparted by the thickening twilight to the massive proportions of the castle, and an air of mysterious vastness hung over the frowning battlements that rose in lofty succession each more massive than the preceding, till they reached the donjon-keep which towered above the rest, portentously gigantic in the indistinctness of the evening dusk. Cheerless and cold seemed the barred casements and the massive gates. No hospitable light streamed forth invitingly from the castle. Black, frowning and lordly, it well typified the morose and churlish soul of its lord.

Entering by the huge postern and passing the successive drawbridges which spanned the several motes dividing the walls, we come at length to the door of the great hall of the castle. Within, the air of such comfort contrasted strikingly, with the cold night that was darkening without. The crackling ash-logs roared on the ample hearth and threw a warm, rich glow on the walls of the long, low hall, gilding the spreading antlers of the-deer and the white gleaming tusks of the wild boar that hung on the wall as ornaments and as trophies, and tipping with golden flame the points of the spears and javelins that had subdued them. In its soft light the outline of the heavy carved furniture was mellowed into a rounder symmetry, and the grotesque forms that graced the chairs and tables were softened into beauty. The group of stag hounds that slept around the hearth, with their long noses thrust between their slender outstretched legs, blended harmoniously with the repose of the scene. At a table which stood on a raised platform at the further end of the hall, three persons were engaged at their evening repast. The central seat was occupied by a tall and powerfully-built man, dressed in a style of some magnificence, but with little taste and less neatness. His mantle was of rich and heavy fabric, much soiled and frayed at the edges and his brown hands were garnished with brilliant jewels and uncut nails. The sprinkled grey of his smoothed hair and the wrinkles sown thickly on his low, broad forehead betrayed alike the ravages of time and passions, and the eye that gleamed beneath his shaggy brows, showed that passing years had left no trace of weakness in his heart. At his right sat a lady whose cold and clear-cut beauty was expressive only of haughty indifference. In the cold glance of the full blue eye, in the self-reliant posture of the graceful head surmounted by a woven coronet of her own golden hair, was exhibited the spirit of defiant independence, which had sprung from the resistance to oppression that her position of a ward rendered necessary. If the good cheer at the right of the baron could not tempt the pensive maiden, that at his left had no reason to complain of like neglect; for a valiant trencherman, whose shaven head and robe of serge left no doubt of his vocation, was doing his "greedy utmost," and the infinite gusto with which he prosecuted his researches into a huge venison pasty showed plainly the gratification he felt in performing his duty of feeding *one* of the lambs of the church.

The baron at length broke a sullen silence that had lasted while the priest with shut eyes was realizing the requisite flavor of a stump of Hock, by saying suddenly to the maiden,

"A mi'night hence Sir Guy de Merval will be here. It is my will that thou conquer thy childish fancy touching this affection and look upon him as my fast friend and thy future lord."

"I shall look on him," answered the maiden quickly, "as the shapeless changeling that he is: a figure like the lame hunchback of Calais and a face like Nero in the hangings. Thou knowest the monkey's mischief, Father Bernard. It was he who laid the addled eggs in thy chair; sent thee a living toad in the shell of a sweet-seeming pasty; and tore up thy precious Virgilius to make fly-traps withal. Finds he favor in *thy* sight?"

The deliberate priest thus appealed to, responded gravely, "Judge not too straitly the pranks of youth. Sir Guy is a devout Knight and a godly and hath promised rich alms to the brothers of St. Benedict when thy broad lands are his."

"May the brethren live till they get them," said the lady laughingly and the impetuous baron cried out, "This talk is vain. Thou shalt wed none but Sir Guy. My word is pledged and it shall not fall for the humours of a girl."

"Nay then," she answered carelessly, "an it please you, rather than be bound to an ape on earth, I will live fancy-free and dying lead apes in the nether world."

"By St. Jude," said the baron, "but I am glad that thou art fancy free in spite of that fair haired stripling Roland de Courcy. I told thee he would soon be forgotten, when he fled with the Lion Heart to Palestine."

"Hast thou forgotten him? or the shout that went up when he sent the ungainly Guy to the dust, and smote him with his lance reversed as he crawled from the lists?"

"I see," said Conrad scornfully, "the boy's white face and fair hair have shared thy foolish heart."

To this taunt the lady Eleanor made no reply. The silent indignation of her curling lip and flashing eye was contradicted by the soft blush that deepened on her cheeks.

"Were this youngster yet in the body," muttered Conrad to himself, "he yet might work me ill. Blessed be the fever that laid him low at Trebigondi."

"Wherefore," said the busy Churchman, "neglect ye this pasty? Herein hath Ralph proved himself a second Apicius and this deer were worthy the arrow of Hubert the Hunter Saint."

"Peace!" said the baron impatiently who had been listening for a moment intently to distant sounds. At that instant there arose without the walls the clear and musical tones of the warder's bugle, above all the clatter of the storm which was beginning in earnest. The savage bark of the mastiff by the gate was repeated by the curs within, till the greyhounds in the hall caught the infection and howled in unison. Scarcely had the tumult subsided when the steward appeared at the door, ushering into the hall a stranger whose tall and graceful frame was enveloped in a dripping cloak. His hat resembled that of a palmer, but a massive silver brooch supplied the place of the cockle-shells in front, and a heavy ostrich feather hung gracefully back from his brow. Conrad advanced with ready courtesy to greet him saying, "Thou art welcome to Mermaison, on a night so churlish whoever thou art. Thy manner and garb betray thy gentle birth and warrant that our hospitality will not be ill-bestowed."

"Thanks for thy courtesy," replied the stranger in a pleasant voice which startled the lady Eleanor from her indifference and kindled a strange eagerness in her blue eyes. "I am glad to be sheltered from the mad storm that hath chased me over the moor, and now howls like a baffled demon at the casements. Yet deem not that a noble partakes thy hospitality, though not all unused to sword and spear my hands are most familiar with a gentler instrument. I am of the gentle craft of minstrels, dowered with the smiles of ladies and the gold of lords." Throwing back his ample cloak and giving his hat to a waiting servant, he disclosed a light green tunic, richly embroidered, with a harp worked in gold at the bottom of each flowing sleeve, and clasped at the throat with a silver bugle. His face, which foreign suns had kissed into gypsy swarthiness wore an expression of careless frankness, and his long brown hair clung moist and wavy around his temples. In his hand he held a harp of small size but of exquisite workmanship curiously inlaid with blushing hearts, darts and flames and other symbols employed in the romantic gallantry of the time.

Though the cordial welcome of the baron was slightly cooled at this discovery of his guest's vocation, he invited him to take his seat at the board, where the lady Eleanor and the priest were still sitting. With an obeisance to the lady and a salutation to the monk he took his seat and was immediately assailed by the solicitations of the reverend epicure who deigned to "commend this pasty to his notice; the scent whereof would have lured St. Simeon from his pillar."

After the minstrel had partaken sparingly of the repast they rose and moved nearer the ample fire. Here Conrad, whose rude straight forwardness acknowledged little restraint from delicacy, said to the minstrel who was gazing absently into the glowing embers, "Sir minstrel, since thou hast thy harp at hand we would be glad to hear some sample of thine art. Music hath but seldom echoed within these walls." The lady who had hitherto remained silent, joined her smiling entreaties and the priest whose dislike to harpers had been overcome by the stranger's commendation of his darling venison expressed his desire to "listen" to the strains wherewith the holy son of Jesse did deliver Saul." At these solicitations the harper bowing lowly said with a smile, "It is your courtesy, fair lady and noble knight, that chooseth to entreat where you might well command."

The fire replenished by the hand of a servant threw its red glow warmly over the hall, tinged with a rosy light the rough rafters and the time-stained walls, and softened into benignity the grim heads of the lions that grinned on the quaint old chairs.

The minstrel after touching carelessly with his silver *wrest* the keys of his harp, said at last, "I will sing, an't please you, a song made by Roland de Courcy a young Knight of Normandy (God rest his soul) when we fought under the Lion Heart in Palestine."

Conrad glanced hastily at Eleanor, to see how she would receive the awful tidings thus suddenly conveyed. But a vague and joyful hope had crept into her heart and she heard not or heeded not the intimation of De Courcy's fate. The brown cheek of the minstrel flushed as he met for a moment her eager glance; and then commenced in a full rich voice the following verses, set to a sweet and mournful melody of Provence:

1

The breezes come gently to me,
As I lie neath the tamarind tree
By my good charger's side, and watch the sails glide
O'er the ripples of blue Galilee.
Yet wildly my weary heart pants
To stray 'mid the lilies of France,
And the vineyards that lie, neath the warm sunny sky
In summer's voluptuous trance.

2

My wild, errant fancy will rove
To the home of the lady I love,
And heavenly dreams, oft bless me with gleams
Of a beauty, all beauty above.
I pine for the light of her eyes,
When the stars o'er Gennesaret rise
In the deep noon of night when the moon's mellow
    light
Is flooding the Syrian skies.

3

I lie 'mid the orient flowers
And remember the desolate hours
And her love in my breast, like the sun in the east
Its glowing light over me showers.
Nor battle, nor pleasure nor toil
Can the sorrow of absence beguile,
And I sigh for the pride, that drove from her side
The heart that but lived in her smile.

As the singer proceeded in his lay his voice which at the beginning had seemed employed only in the careless display of its own powers, gradually gathered a deeper tone of feeling and poured out the concluding lines in the full and tremulous utterances of uncontrolled passion. The lady, whose attention had been riveted by the voice of the stranger, sat with rapt eagerness drinking in each cadence of the music, while the eloquent blushes flashed like reddish streams to her face, tinging with delicate crimson her cheek and brow. In a tumult of passionate confusion she buried her burning face in her white hands nor ventured to raise her eyes till the last echo of the song died tremblingly away. Then she raised her head and glanced around suddenly with a quick misgiving, to search for any token of suspicion in the faces of the others. But the baron was gazing calmly with half-shut eyes at the embers and the priest was placidly rubbing his shaven poll.

"A marvellous good song," said Conrad, who in truth had not heard a word of it, despising in his soul the effusions of the lovesick versifiers who had lately deluged Europe with Provencal rhymes and tunes.

"Marvellously well sung," chimed in the monk, who holding it his duty to appreciate the music, had been beating the time with his fat finger, though considering the words sinfully light and trivial.

"One of thy skill," resumed the baron, "must needs have no lack of employment. But if it suits thy fancy we would reward thee well if thou wilt abide with us till St. Agnes Eve, that thou mightst make merry our wedding guests with thy harp and song." "St. Anthony save us," whispered the monk to the baron, "a juggling harper in the castle for a moon of days. The quiet of the household will be changed for the tinkling of vile tunes and the tones of unholy ribaldry will chime in with our masses. Bethink thee too, minstrels were ever huge feeders. Thy choice wine of Cyprus will vanish at his thirsty touch like the fountain of Lorelli at the bidding of St. Anselm."

"Peace! I shall follow my humour," said Conrad and awaited his answer. At the mention of the approaching nuptials, the minstrel had cast a furtive glance full of anxious curiosity at Eleanor but seemed reassured by the kindling indignation in her eye. She replied with dignity, "Nay my lord, it avails not to bid minstrels to that banquet. If thou art determined so am I. Sir Guy will that day wed but a cold bride and I shall be listening to the harpings of the shining ones ere that wedding-day dawns."

"Wilt stay, or no?" said Conrad.

"It grieves me," said the minstrel, "to leave this goodly castle and this fair company, but I have pledged my word to be with my liege King Richard ere St. Prisca's festival. Were he simply a King, I would gladly neglect him for you; but he joins to his royal graces the greater dignity of a Provencal troubadour and commands us by his love, as brothers in the craft. I have hasted from the South since sabbath-eve and have met these northern storms which have held me a day from the ship that waits me at Calais."

"Who art thou then, that comest from the south, and speakest the manly accents of Normandy as purely as thou hadst grown up beneath the towers of Rouen."

For a moment the minstrel hesitated but suddenly rejoined, "My mother (the rest of heaven be hers!) was of Normandy and by her my tongue was early trained to the manly roughness of the Norman speech. Your hospitality demands my name and lineage. I am called Fouquet de Marseilles." The priest roused by the name exclaimed, "By St. Denis, but I should know thy father. Thou art most unlike him or else the suns of Palestine have changed thee sorely. Hast thou ever seen the scar that

Otto the Keeper planted on his left temple when we shot the leverets in his park?"

"Oftentimes," said the minstrel nervously, evidently desirous to change the subject which the priest seemed willing to continue, as he shook his head sadly, saying, "wild days—wild days." The minstrel anxious to escape further reminiscences, began to touch his harp to a lively prelude, saying, "An't please you, noble sir, I will sing a song more becoming a warrior's ear, about the exploits of Count Robert of Tremaine, and I hope to please you most holy father with praising separately the eleven thousand Virgins of Cologne." And he forthwith began the recital of those ponderous romances which the monks had lately brought into the courts in which a commonplace hero was led through absurd impossibilities in search of an indefinite good, the whole mingled with distorted scraps of learning and with extracts from the calendar which almost justified his extravagant promise to the monk. As he proceeded singing in a droning voice the dullest of tales to the sleepiest of tunes, the baron shut his eyes the better to hear and the priest was not slow in following his example. As the minstrel still plied his soothing art, the fire, the combined, brought the pair to such a state of somnolent satisfaction that their nasal notes of contentment began to mingle discordantly with the song. When his object was thus accomplished, the minstrel turning quickly to the lady, began with a changed voice and manner to sing to the same measure the following song, while the Cerberean pair still snored happily unconscious:

I

Young Roland fled to the Holy Land,
To fight 'neath the cross with the Paynim band.
His trust in his arm and God above

His hope, the smile of his lady-love.

II

His arm was strong and his steed was good,
His blade drank deep of the moslem blood.
And the King said, "Well thy spurs thou'st won
And dubbed him Knight at Askalon.

III

Away to his native land he hied
To claim the hand of his peerless bride.
But he found that a dastard, vile and old
Was to wed fair Eleanor's lands and gold.

IV

So alone he entered the baron's hall
He baffled the eyes of the warders all.
He bore her away from her native land
For love was free on the English strand.

As he concluded he rose and approaching her said in a low rapid tone, "Wilt thou trust me? Lay thy fate in my hands and all shall be well."

"Roland," she cried violently agitated, "Rash presumptions, forbear. If they should wake——"

The priest at this moment roused by the cessation of the music, opened his round eyes and sighed sleepily, "Master Minstrel, I commend your song. The recital of the dream of St. Dunstan proves thee ready of tongue and devout of heart."

"The devil of slumber hast bound my temples with poppies and filled my eyes with sand," growled the baron. "Let us seek our beds. Wilt thou not remain with us a little space?"

"I must be far hence ere the dawn," rejoined the minstrel, "and will but strain your kindness for one of these skins and a place by the hearth."

"Pierre," roared Conrad till a warder entered. "See

that the minstrel depart as early as he will without let or hindrance." Low doors on either side of the great hall led to the different sleeping apartments. The lady retired first and as she closed the door the baron coolly fastened it on the outside with a rude bolt and did the same with the monk. Then turning to the minstrel, "Small thanks for small courtesy, sir rhymer. If thou wert wise, thou wouldst have been the friend of Conrad. But since thou wilt then depart in God's name with peace between us." Handing him a small purse and waiting for no reply he strode to his chamber. The minstrel wrapped a bearskin loosely round and lay down by the chimney. The fire was dying on the hearth. Its dull flame glimmered on the darkening furniture; and in the corners of the hall the shadows were deepening and spectral forms seemed coming and going in the gloom as if the spirit of darkness were rustling its black plumes. The minstrel gazed now at the flickering firelight, now at the thronging shadows, and at last the room seemed gliding from his swimming eyes, and the leaden hand of sleep was pressing down his eyelids, when the cold nose of one of the stag hounds, was thrust into his face, dispelling at once his dreams and his drowsiness. "Fool!" he muttered, "when the goal of my life is before to sleep away the precious moments. Love and fortune have favored me wondrously. *Adite, o superni*, as father Lawrence used to say when he cared not to help himself." He rose cautiously and walked across the rush strewn floor. Glancing round he saw no moving thing but his own gaunt shadow flickering on the wall. Going up to the door of the lady Eleanor's apartment, he shot the bolt back noiselessly and whispered gently, "Eleanor." No reply. He repeated the call, "Beshrew the slumber that lights on all this night." He was about to enter in his desperation when the door opened and the lady stood before him. Her dress had not been disarranged and the traces of agitation were plainly betrayed by the flushed cheek and the feverish sparkle of her eye. She began in a hurried and trembling whisper, "What dost thou here Roland? the blind error of Conrad cannot last. His very dogs thirst for thy blood. Thou art tempting thy fate."

"Hate hath not eyes like love," answered the minstrel quietly.

"Fly even now! the doors are open to thee. Thou art not safe till the sea divides ye twain."

"Canst thou think, Eleanor, that I would fly alone; deserting the joy that hath been through weary years the star of my hope and the heaven of my prayers: that hath guarded me like the shield of a mother's blessing in the midst of wild vice and revelry and hath nerved my arm like a talisman when carnage raged around me. If thou wilt share my flight the dawn will see leagues of safety between us and thy tyrant. If thou refuse, my life's light is quenched and we will wash out our hate in blood beneath the walls of Mermaison. Now thou shalt choose. Thou art my fate. Be my angel also."

As Roland was speaking, all the irresolute perplexity of the lady vanished and the light of a new purpose dawned peacefully in her clear blue eyes. She turned to Roland, and the dying firelight shone brightly-reflected in her gushing tears, and touched into tenderer beauty the struggling roses on her cheeks as she laid her soft hand in the palm of the knight, and murmured so low that the ear of love alone could catch the tremulous sweetness of the tones, "Thine to the world's end whatever betide."

"Holy Lady of Bethlehem, I thank thee," said Roland reverently, "that life is precious to me again.

He hastily wrapped around her form his cloak which

had been drying by the fire, and threw over his own shoulders the skin which had been his bed, while the lady pacified the awakened hound who was gazing on the scene with bewildered curiosity. He seized his harp and they passed from the hall as silent as their shadows.

The storm had spent its fury and the moon was struggling through the clouds. They proceeded without interruption to the outer gate, where Roland roused the snoring warder who stumbled out from his little hut, and let down the clattering drawbridge. But as they were starting out, he remarked the minstrel's companion and laughed broadly. "How now, Master Harper. Thou dost enter alone—and depart double. Thy suit hath prospered in the kitchen. Whom have thy songs beguiled?" he asked, seizing the arm of the terrified Eleanor. As the moonlight dimly struck her features, the astonished serf cried out, "Hath the devil bewitched me? My lady!" And gazing at the pair with stupid wonder, he raised his horn to strike the impudent minstrel, but before he could bring into action his unwieldy strength, a lightning-like blow from the harp of Roland laid him sprawling senseless on the ground. Snatching the horn of the prostrate giant he blew a shrill flourish and stepping across the drawbridge they saw a speck of shadow detach itself from a clump of trees at a distance and move rapidly towards them over the plain. As it came nearer, it assumed the form of two powerful horses, one bearing a groom in dripping garments, and the other led. Seizing the latter Roland cried to the groom, "Delay not, Hubert. Hasten to the bark. Prepare all sails for England. Fly, or we shall yet override you." He swung the lady to the crupper and vaulted into the saddle. Obedient to a word the charger sprang forward like an arrow and the knight cried gaily, "A league to the sea. Then ho! for England and the court of my liege, a laugh at the rage of Conrad and Guy and a quarrel with Fouquot the Marseillais for the name I stole. How the strings of my harp rattled when I smote the warder! I was loth to lose it though. I would fain sing one more song before I lay off the minstrel for the knight and call it "The triumphs of music—over hearts and heads."

The prostrate warder slowly gathered himself up and rubbing his bushy head and gradually realized the state of affairs as he muttered, "Body of me, what a bump is this. I have not had a thump like that since lame Hubert rapped me over the sconce with his crutch at the fair at Calais. Who'd dream a harping springal could hit like that? Gone off with my lady, too. But what seek I? I had Conrad's orders for it. He'll stagger the blessed sun tomorrow with his curses. By 'r Lady of Rouen but the harper has left his tool. I will save it till the Jew Levi comes up at Lammas-tide. Mayhap he will give me for it a piece of gold or at meanest, a jar of his marvellous ointment of Damascus. How Conrad will storm tomorrow. I will tell him it happened after moonset and so 'scape with few bruises."

The Life-Magnet

["The Life-Magnet" is a curiosity of what may be called "co-authorship." A cross between a Poe-like tale of madness and a Mary Shelleyean story of experimental science, its plot was invented by Hay, but the story itself was written out by one of Hay's fellow workers in the U.S. Department of State. "I write today, to ask you to look at a little nightmare in the August *Putnam's* [1870, 6: 152-62]," boasted Hay, "I confess I was greatly tickled with it. He [Alvey A. Adee] wrote it after about fifteen minutes dictation from me, as to the general run of the story.]

There was something about the wholesome sleepiness of Freiberg, in Saxony, that fitted well with the lazy nature of Ronald Wyde. So, having run down there to spend a day or two among the students and the mines, and taking a liking to the quaint, unmodernized town, he bodily changed his plans of autumn-travel, gave up a cherished scheme of Russian vagabondage, had his baggage sent from Dresden, and made ready to settle down and drowse away three or four months in idleness and not over-arduous study. And this move of his led to the happening of a very strange and seemingly unreal event in his life.

Ronald Wyde was then about twenty-five or six years old, rather above the medium height, with thick blue-black hair that he had an artist-trick of allowing to ripple down to this neck, dark hazel eyes that were almost too deeply recessed in their bony orbits, and a troublesome growth of beard that, close-shaven as he always was, showed in strong blue outline through the thin and rather sallow skin. His address was singularly pleasing, and his wide experience of life, taught him by years of varied travel, made him a good deal of a cosmopolitan in his views and ways, which caused him to be looked upon as a not over-safe companion for young men of his own age or under.

Having made up his mind to winter in Freiberg, his first step was to quit the little hotel, with its mouldy stone-vaulted entrance and its columned dining-room, under whose full-centered arches close beery and smoky fumes lingered persistently, and seek quieter student-lodgings in the heart of the town. His choice was mainly influenced by a thin-railed balcony, twined through and through by the shoots of a vigorous Virginia creeper, that flamed and flickered in the breezy October sunsets in strong relief against the curtains that drifted whitely out and in through the open window. So, with the steady-going and hale old Frau Spritzkrapfen he took up his quarters, fully persuading himself that he did so for the sake of the stray home-breaths that seemed to stir the scarlet vine-leaves more gently for him, and ignoring pretty Lottchen's great, earnest Saxon eyes as best he could.

A sunny morning followed his removal to Frau Spritzkrapfen's tidy home. There had been a slight rain in the early night, and the footways were yet bright and moist in patches that the slanting morning rays were slowly coaxing away. Ronald Wyde, having set his favorite books handily on the dimity-draped table, which comprised for him the process of getting to rights, and having given more than one glance of amused wonderment at the naive blue-and-white scriptural tiles that cased his cumbrous four-story earthenware stove, and smiled lazily at poor Adam's obvious and sudden indigestion, even while the uneaten half-apple remained in his guilty hand, he stepped out on his balcony, leaned his elbows among the crimson leaves, and took in the healthful morning air in great draughts. It was a Sunday; the bells of the gray minster hard by were iterating their clanging calls to the simple townsfolk to come and be droned to in sleepy German gutturals from the carved, pillar-hung pulpit inside. Looking down, he saw thick-ankled women cluttering past in loose wooden-soled shoes, annoying dumpy girls with tow-braids primly dangling to their hips, convoying sturdy Dutch-built luggers of younger brothers up the easy slope that led to the church and the bells. Presently Frau Spritzkrapfen and dainty Lottchen, rosy with soap and health, slipped through the doorway beneath him out into the little church-bound throng, and, as they disappeared, left the house and street somehow unaccountably alone. Feeling this, Ronald Wyde determined on a stroll.

Something in the Sabbath stillness around him led Ronald away from the swift clang and throbbing hum of the bells and in the direction of the old cemetery. Passing through the clumsy tower-gate that lifts its grimy bulk sullenly, like a huge head-stone over the grave of a dead time of feudalism, he reached the burial-ground and entered the quiet enclosure. The usual touching reverence of the Germans for their dead was strikingly manifest around him. The humbler mounds, walled up with rough stones a foot or two above the pathway level, carried on their crests little gardens of gay and inexpensive plants; while on the tall wooden crosses at their head hung yellow wreaths, half hiding the hopeful legend, "Wiedersehen." The more pretentious slabs bore vases filled with fresh flowers; while in the grate-barred vaults, that skirted the ground like the arches of a cloister, lay rusty heaps of long-since mouldered bloom, topped by newer wreaths tossed lovingly in to wilt and turn to dust in their turn, like those cast in before them in memory of that other dust asleep below.

Turning aside from the central walk that halved the cemetery, Ronald strolled along, his hands in his pockets, his eyes listlessly fixed on the orange-colored fumes and rolling smoke that welled out of tall chimneys in the hollow beyond, an idle student-tune humming on his lips, and his thought nowhere, and everywhere, at once. Happening to look away from the dun smoke-trail for an instant, he found something of greater interest close at hand. An old man stooped stiffly over a simple mound, busied among the flowers that hid it, and by his side crouched a young girl, perhaps fourteen years old, who peered up at Ronald with questioning, velvet-brown eyes. The old man heard the intruder's steps crunching in the damp gravel, and slowly looked up too.

"Good morning, mein Herr," said Ronald, pleasantly.

The old man remained for an instant blinking nervously, and shading his eyes from the full sunlight that fell on his face. A quiet face it was, and very old, seamed and creased by mazy wrinkles that played at aimless cross-purposes with each other, beginning and ending nowhere. His thick beard and thin, curved nose looked just a little Jewish, and seemed at variance with his pale blue eyes that were still bright in spite of age. And yet, bearded as he was, there was a lurking expression about his features that bordered upon effeminacy, and made the treble of his voice sound even more thin and womanish as he answered Wyde's greeting.

"Good morning, too, mein Herr. A stranger to our town, I see."

"Yes; but soon not to be called one, I hope. I am here

for the winter."

"A cold season—a cold season; our northern winters are very chilling to an old man's 'blood.'" And slouching together into a tired stoop, he resumed his simple task of knotting a few flowers into a clumsy nosegay. Ronald stood and watched him with a vague interest. Presently, the flowers being clumped to his liking, the old man pried himself upright by getting a good purchase with his left hand in the small of his back, and so deliberately that Ronald almost fancied he heard him creak. The girl rose too, and drew her thin shawl over her shoulders.

"You Germans love longer than we," said Ronald, glancing at the flowers that trembled in the old man's bony fingers, and then downwards to the quiet grave; "a lifetime of easy-going love and a year or two of easier-forgetting are enough for us."

"Should I forget my own flesh and blood?" asked the old man, simply.

Ronald paused, a moment, and, pointing downwards, said:

"Your daughter, then I fancy?"

"Yes."

"Long dead?"

"Very long; more than fifty years."

Ronald stared, but said nothing audibly. Inwardly he whispered something about being devilish glad to make the wandering Jew's acquaintance, rattled the loose gröschen in his pocket, and turned to follow the tottering old man and firm-footed child down the walk. After a dozen paces they halted before a more ambitious tombstone, on which Ronald could make out the well-remembered name of Plattner. The child took the flowers and laid them reverently on the stone.

"It seems to me almost like arriving at the end of a

pilgrimage," said Ronald, "when I stand by the grave of a man of science. Perhaps you knew him, mein Herr?"

"He was my pupil."

"Whew!" thought Ronald, "that makes my friend here a centenarian at least."

"My pupil and friend," the feeble voice went on; "and, more than that, my daughter's first lover, and only one."

"*Ach so!*" drawled Ronald.

"And now, on her death-day, I take these poor flowers from her to him, as I have done all these years."

Something in the pathetic earnestness of his companion touched Ronald Wyde, and he forthwith took his hands out of his pockets, and didn't try to whistle inaudibly—which was a great deal for him to do.

"I know Plattner well by his works," he said; "I once studied mineralogy for nearly a month."

"You love science, then?"

"Yes; like everything else, for diversion."

"It was different with him," quavered the old man, pointing unsteadily to the head-stone. "Science grew to be his one passion, and many discoveries rewarded him for his devotion. He was groping on the track of a far greater achievement when he died."

"May I ask what it was?" said Ronald, now fairly interested.

"The creation and isolation of the principle of Life!"

This was too much for Ronald Wyde; down dived his restless hands into his trowser's pockets again, and the gröschen rattled as merrily as before.

"I have made quite a study of biology, and all that sort of thing," said he; "and, although a good deal of a skeptic, and inclined to follow Huxley, I can't bring myself to conceive of life without organism. Such theorizing is, to my mind, on a par with the illogical search for the philosopher's stone and a perpetual motor."

The old man's eyes sparkled as he turned full upon Ronald.

"You dismiss the subject very airily, my young friend," he cried; "but let me tell you that I—I, whom you see here—have grappled with such problems through a weary century, and have conquered one of them."

"And that one is—"

"The one that conquered Plattner!"

"Do I understand you to claim that you have discovered the life-principle?"

"Yes."

"Will you permit an utter stranger to inquire what is its nature?"

"Certainly. It is twofold. The ultimate principle of life is carbon; the cause of its combination with water, or rather with the two gaseous elements of water, and the development of organized existence therefrom, is electricity."

Ronald Wyde shrugged his broad shoulders a little, and absently replied,

"All I can say, mein Herr, is, that you've got the bulge on me."

"I beg your pardon—"

"Excuse me; I unconsciously translated an Americanism. I mean that I don't quite understand you."

"Which means that you do not believe me. It is but natural at your age, when one doubts as if by instinct. Would you be convinced?"

"Nothing would please me better."

With the same painful effort as before, the old man straightened himself and made a piercing clairvoyant examination into and through Ronald Wyde's eyes, as if reading the brain beyond them.

"I think I can trust you," he mumbled at last. "Come with me."

Leaning on the young girl's arm, the old philosopher faltered through the cemetery and into the town, followed by Wyde, his hands again pocketed for safety. Groups of released church-goers, sermon-fed, met them, and once in a while some stout burgher would nod patronizingly to Ronald's guides, and get in response a shaky, sidelong roll of the old man's head, as if it were mounted on a weak spiral spring. Further on they intersected a knot of students, who eyed them askance and exchanged remarks in an undertone. Keeping on deeper into the foul heart of the town, they passed through swarms of idle children playing sportlessly, as poverty is apt to play, in the dank shadows of the narrow street. They seemed incited to mirth and ribaldry by the sight of Ronald's new friend, and one even ventured to hurl a clod at him; but this striking Ronald instead, and he facing promptly to the hostile quarter from whence it came, caused a sudden slinking of the crowd into unknown holes, like a horde of rats, and the street was for a time empty save for the little party that threaded it. Ronald began to think that the old man's sanity was gravely called in doubt by the townsfolk, and would readily have backed out of his adventure but for the curiosity that had now got the upper hand of him.

Presently the old man sidled into a dingy doorway, like a tired beast run to earth, and Ronald followed him, not without a wish that the architect had provided for a more efficient lighting of the sombre passage-way in which he found himself. A sharp turn to the right after a dozen groping-paces, a narrow stairway, a bump or two against unexpected saliences of rough mortared wall, two steps upward and one very surprising step downward through a cavernous doorway that took away Ronald's breath for a moment, and sent it back again with a hot, creeping wave of sudden perspiration all over him, as is the way with missteps, and two more sharp turns, brought the three into a black no-thoroughfare of a hall, whose further end was closed by a locked door. The girl here rubbed a brimstone abomination of a match into a mal-odorous green glow, and by its help the old man got a tortuous key into the snaky opening in the great lock, creakily shot back its bolt, swung open the door, and motioned Ronald to enter.

He found himself in a long and rather narrow room, with a high ceiling, duskily lighted by three wide windows that were thickly webbed and dusted, like ancestral bottles of fine crusty Port. A veritable den it was, filled with what seemed to be the wrecks of philosophical apparatus dating back two or three generations—ill-fated ventures on the treacherous main of science. Here a fat-bellied alembic lolled lazily over in a gleamy sand-bath, like a beach-lost galleon at ebb-tide; and there a heap of broken porcelain-tubing and shards of crucibles lay like bleaching ship-ribs on a sullen shore. Beyond, by the middle window, stood a furnace, fire-less, and clogged with gray ashes. Two or three solid old-time tables, built when joiners were more lavish of oaken timber than nowadays, stood hopelessly littered with retorts, filtering funnels, lamps, ringstands, and squat-beakers of delicate glass, caked with long-dried sediment, all alike dust-smirched. Ronald involuntarily sought for some huge Chaldaic tome, conveniently open at a favorite spell, or a handy crocodile or two dangling from the square beams overhead, but saw nothing more formidable than a stray volume of "Kant's Critique of Pure Reason." Taking this up and glancing at its fly-leaf, he saw a name written in spidery German script, almost illegible from its shakiness—"Max Lebensfunke."

"Your name?" he asked.

"Yes, mein Herr," answered the old man, taking the volume and caressing it like a live thing in his fumbling hands. "This book was given to me by the great Kant himself," he added.

Reverently replacing it, he advanced a few steps towards the middle of the room. Ronald followed, and, turning away from the windows, looked further around him. In striking contrast to the undisturbed disorder, so redolent of middle-age alchemy, was the big table that flanked the laboratory through its whole length. It began with a powerful galvanic battery, succeeded by a wiry labyrinth of coils and helices, with little keys in front of them like a telegraph-office retired from business; these gave place to many-necked jars wired together by twos and threes, like oath-bound patriots plotting treason; beyond them stood a great glass globe, connected with a sizable air-pump, and filled with a complexity of shiny wires and glassware; next loomed up a huge induction-magnet, carefully insulated on solid glass supports; and at the further extremity of the table lay—a corpse.

Ronald Wyde, in spite of his many-sided experience of dissection-rooms, and morgues, and other ghastlinesses to which he had long since accustomed himself from principle, drew back at the sight—perhaps because he had come to this strange place to clutch the world-old mystery of the life-essence, and found himself, instead, confronted on its threshold by the equal mystery of death.

Herr Lebensfunke smiled feebly at this movement.

"A subject received this morning from Berlin," he

said, in answer to Wyde's look of inquiry. "A sad piece of extravagance, mein Herr—a luxury to which I can rarely afford to treat myself."

Ronald Wyde bent over the body and looked into its face. A rough, red face, that had seemingly seen forty years of low-lived dissipation. The blotched skin and bleary eyes told of debauchery and drunkenness, and a slight alcoholic foetidness was unpleasantly perceptible, as from the breath of one who sleeps away the effects of a carouse.

"I hope you don't think of restoring this soaked specimen to life?" said Ronald.

"That is still beyond me," answered the old man, mournfully. "As yet I have not created life of a higher grade than that of the lowest zoöphytes."

"Do you claim to have done as much as that?"

"It is not an idle claim," said Herr Lebensfunke, solemnly. "Look at this, if you doubt."

"This" was the great crystal globe that rose from the middle of the long table, and dominated its lesser accessories, as some great dome swells above the clustered houses of a town. Tubes passing through its walls met in a smaller central globe half filled with a colorless liquid. Beneath this, and half encircling it, was an intricate maze of bright wire; and two other wires dipped into it, touching the surface of the liquid with their platinum tips. Within the liquid pulsed a shapeless mass of almost transparent spongy tissue.

"You see an aggregation of cells possessed of life—of a low order, it is true, but none the less life," said the philosopher, proudly. "These were created from water chemically pure, with the exception of a trace of ammonia, and impregnated with liquid carbon, by the combined action of heat and induced electricity, in vacuo.

Look!"

He pressed one of the keys before him. Presently the wire began to glow with a faint light, which increased in intensity till the coil flamed into pure whiteness. Removing his finger, the current ceased to flow, and the wire grew rapidly cool.

"I passed the whole strength of sixty cups through it to show you its action. Ordinarily, with one or two carbon cells, and refining the current by triple induction, the temperature is barely blood-warm.

"Pardon an interruption," said Ronald. "You spoke of liquid carbon; does it exist?"

"Yes; here is some in this phial. See it—how pure, how transparent! how it loves and hoards the light!" The old man held the phial up as he spoke, and turned it round and round. "See how it flashes! No wonder, for it is the diamond, liquid and uncrystallized. Think how these fools of men have called diamonds precious above all gems through these many weary years, and showered them on their kings, or tossed them to their mistresses' feet, never dreaming that the silly stone they lauded was inert, crystallized life!"

"Can't you crystallize diamonds yourself?" asked Wyde, "and make Freiberg a Golconda and yourself a Croesus?"

"It could be done, after the lapse of thousands of years," replied Herr Lebensfunke. "Place undiluted liquid carbon in that inner globe, keep the coil at a white heat, and if Adam had started the process, his heir-at-law would have a koh-i-noor to-day, and a nice lawsuit for its possession."

Ronald Wyde bent toward the globe once more and examined the throbbing mass closely, whistling softly meanwhile.

"If you can create this cellular life, why not develop it still higher into an organism?"

"Because I can only create life—not soul. Years ago I was a freethinker, now my discoveries have made me a deist; for I found that my cells, living as they were, and possessing undoubted parietal circulation, were not germs; and though they might cluster into a bulk like this, as bubbles do to form froth, to evolve an animal or plant from them was far beyond me; that needs what we call soul. But, in searching blindly for this higher power, I grasped a greater discovery than any I had hoped for—the power to isolate life from its bodily organism."

"You have to keep the bottle carefully corked, I should imagine," laughed Ronald.

"Not quite," said Herr Lebensfunke, joining in the laugh. "Life is not glue. My grand discovery is the life-magnet."

"Which has the post of honor on your table here, has it not?" inquired Ronald, drawing his hand from his pocket and pointing to the insulated coil.

The old man glanced keenly at his hand as he did so; at which Ronald seemed confused, and pocketed it again abruptly.

"Yes, that is the life-magnet. You see this bent glass tube surrounded by the helix? That tube contains liquid carbon. I pass through the helix a current of induced electricity, generated by the action of these sixty Bunsen cups upon a succession of coils with carbon cores, and the magnet becomes charged with soulless life. I reverse the stream—what was positive now is negative, and the same magnet will absorb life from a living being to an extent only to be measured by thousands of millions."

"Then, what effect is produced on the body you pump the life from?"

"Death."

"And what becomes of the soul?"

"I don't quite know. I fancy, however, that the magnet absorbs that too."

"Can it give it back?"

"Certainly; otherwise my life-magnet would belie its name, and be simply an ingenious and expensive instrument of death. By reversing the conditions, I can restore both soul and life to the body from which I drew them, or to another body, even after the lapse of several days."

"Have you ever done so?"

"I have."

Ronald looked reflectively downward to his boot-toe, but seemed to find nothing there—except a boot-toe.

"I say, my friend," he spoke at last, "haven't you got a pin you can stick in me? I'd like to know if I'm dreaming."

"I can convince you better than by pins," replied Herr Lebensfunke. "Let me see that hand you hide so carefully."

Ronald Wyde slowly drew it from his pocket, as reluctantly as though it were a grudged charity dole, and extended it to the old man. Its little finger was gone.

"A defect that I am foolishly sensitive about," said he. "A childish freak—playing with edged tools, you know. A boy-playmate chopped it off by accident: I cut his head open with his own hatchet, and made an idiot of him for life—that's all."

"I could do this," said Herr Lebensfunke, pausing on each word as if it were somewhat heavy, and had to be lifted out of his cramped chest by force; "I could draw your entity into that magnet, leaving you side by side with this corpse. I could dissect a finger from that same corpse, attach it to your own dead hand by a little of that palpitating life-mass you have seen, pass an electric stream through it, and a junction would be effected in three or four days. I could then restore you to existence, whole, and not maimed as now."

"I don't quite like the idea of dying, even for a day," answered Wyde. "Couldn't you contrive to lend me a body while you are mending my own?"

"You can take that one, if you like."

Ronald Wyde looked once more at the sodden features of the corpse, and smiled lugubriously.

"A mighty shabby old customer," he said, "and I doubt if I could feel at home in his skin; but I'm willing to risk it for the sake of the novelty of the thing."

The old philosopher's thin face lit up with pleasure.

"You consent, then?" he chuckled in his womanish treble.

"Of course I do. Begin at once, and have done with it."

"Not now, mein Herr; some modifications must be made in the connections—mere matters of detail. Come again to-night."

"At what hour?"

"At ten. Mein Vögelein, show the Herr the way out."

The girl, who had been moving restlessly about the room all this time, with her wild brown eyes fixed now on Ronald, now on the old man, and oftener in a shy, inquisitive stare on the corpse, lit a dusty chemical lamp and led the way down the awkward passages and stairs. Ronald tried to start a conversation with her as he followed.

"You are too young, my birdling, to be accustomed to such sights as this upstairs."

"Birdling is not too young, she's almost fourteen," said the girl, proudly. "And she likes it, too; it makes her think of mother. Mother went to sleep on that table, mein Herr."

"Poor thing! she's half-witted," thought Wyde as he passed into the street. "By-by, birdie."

Home he walked briskly, to be met under his flaming balcony by Lottchen's kindly afternoon greeting. How had mein Herr passed his Sabbath? she asked.

"Quietly enough, Lottchen. I met an old philosopher in the God's Acre, and went home with him to his shop. Have you ever heard of Herr Doctor Lebensfunke?"

"Yes, mein Herr. Wrong here, they say"; and she tapped her wide, round German forehead, and lifted her eyes expressively heavenward.

"Sold himself to the devil, eh?" asked Wyde.

Lottchen was not quite sure on that point. Some said one thing, and some another. There was undoubtedly a devil, else how could good Doctor Luther have thrown his inkstand at him? But he had never been seen in Doctor Lebensfunke's neighborhood; and, on the whole, Lottchen was inclined to attribute the Herr Doctor's trouble to an indefinable something whose nature was broadly hinted at by more tapping of the forehead.

Ronald Wyde mounted the stairs, locked himself in his room, and wished himself out of the scrape he was getting into. But, being in for it now, he lit a cigar, and tried to fancy the processes he would have to go through, and how he, a natty and respectable young fellow, would look and feel in a drunkard's skin. His conjectures being too foggily outlined to please him, he put them aside, and waited impatiently enough for ten o'clock.

A moonlight walk through the low streets, transfigured by the silver gleam into fairy vista—all but the odor—brought him to Herr Lebensfunke's house. Simple birdling, on the lookout for him, piloted him through the unsafe channel, and brought him to anchor in the dimly-lit room.

"All is ready," said the philosopher, as he trembled forward and shook Ronald's hand. "See here." Zig-zags of silk-bound wire squirmed hither and thither from the life-magnet. Two of them ended in carbon points. "And here, too, my young friend, is your new finger."

It lay, detached, in the central globe, and on its severed end atoms of protoplasm were already clustered. "Literally a second-hand article," thought Ronald; but, not venturing to translate the idiom, he only bowed and said, "*Ach so!*" which means anything and everything, in German.

It was not without a very natural sinking of the heart that Ronald Wyde divested himself of his clothing, and took his position, by the old man's direction, on the stout table, side by side with the dead. A flat brass plate pressed between his shoulders, and one of the carbon points, clamped in a little insulated stand, rested on his bosom and quivered with the quickened motion of the heart beneath it. The other point touched the dead man's breast.

"Are you ready?"

"Yes."

The old man pressed a key, and as he did so a sharp sting, hardly worse than a leech's bite, pricked Ronald Wyde's breast. A sense of languor crept slowly upon him, his feet tingled, his breath came slowly, and waves of light and shade pulsed in indistinct alternation before his sight; but through them the old man's eyes peered into his, like a dream. Presently Ronald would have started if he could, for two old philosophers were craning over him instead of one. But as he looked more steadily, one face softly dimmed into nothing, and the other grew brighter and stronger in its lines, while the room flushed with an unaccountable light. The little key clicked once more; a vague sensation that the current had somehow ceased to flow, roused him, and he raised himself on his elbow and looked in blank bewilderment at his own dead self lying by his side in the daylight, while the sunrise tried to peer through the webbed panes.

"Is it over?" he asked, with a puzzled glance around him; and added, "Which am I?"

"Either or both," answered" Herr Lebensfunke. "Your identity will be something of a problem to you for a day or two."

Aided by the old man, Ronald awkwardly got into the sleazy clothes that went with the exchange—growing less and less at home each minute. He felt weak and sore; his head ached, and the wound left by the fresh amputation of his little finger throbbed angrily.

"I suppose I may as well go now," he said. "When can I get my own self there back again?"

"On Thursday night, if all works well," said the old man. "Till then, good-day."

Ronald Wyde's first impulse, as he shambled into the open air, was to go home; but he thought of the confusion his sadly-mixed identity would cause in Frau Spritzkrapfen's quiet household, and came to a dead stop to consider the matter. Then he decided to quit the town for the interminable four days—to go to Dresden, or anywhere. His next step was to slouch into the nearest beer-cellar and call for beer, pen, and paper. While waiting for these, he purveyed his own reflection in the dingy glass that hung above the table he sat by—a glass that gave his face a wavy look, as if seen through heated air. He felt an amused pride in his altered appearance, much as a masquerader might be pleased with a clever disguise, and caught himself wondering whether he were likely to be recognized in it. Apparently satisfied of his safety from detection, he turned to the table and wrote a beer-scented note to Frau Spritzkraphen, explaining his sudden absence by some discreet fiction. He got along well enough till he reached the end, when, instead of his own flowing sign-manual, he tipsily scrawled the unfamiliar name of Hans Kraut. Tearing the sheet angrily across, he wrote another, and signed his name with an effort. He was about to seek a messenger to carry his note, when it occurred to him to leave it himself, which he did; and had thereby the keen satisfaction of hearing pretty Lottchen confess, with a blush on her fair German cheek, that they would all miss Herr Wyde very much, because they all loved him. Turning away with a sigh that was very like a hiccough, he trudged to the railway-station and took a ticket to Dresden, going third-class as best befitting his clothes and appearance.

He felt ashamed enough of himself as the train rumbled over the rolling land between Freiberg and the capital, and gave him time to think connectedly over what had happened, and what he now was. His fellow-passengers cast him sidelong looks, and gave him a wide berth. Even the quaint, flat-arched windows of one pane each, that winked out of the red-tiled roofs like sleepy eyes, seemed to leer drunkenly at him as they scudded by.

Ronald Wyde's account of those days in Dresden was vague and misty. He crept along the bustling streets of that sombre, gray city, that seemed to look more natural by cloud-light than in the full sunshine, feeling continually within him a struggle between the two incompatible natures now so strangely blended. Each day he kept up the contest manfully, passing by the countless beer-cellars and drinking-booths with an assumption of firmness and resolution that oozed slowly away toward nightfall, when the animal body of the late Hans Kraut would contrive to get the better of the animating principle of Ronald Wyde; the refined nature would yield to the toper's brute-craving, with an awful sense of its deep degradation in so succumbing, and, before midnight, Hans was gloriously drunk, to Ronald's intense grief.

Time passed somehow. He had memories of sunny lounges on the Bruhl'aghe Terrace, looking on the turbid flow of the eddied Elbe, and watching the little steamboats that buzzed up and down the city's flanks, settling now and then, like gad-flies, to drain it of a few drops of its human life. Well-known friends, whose hands he had grasped not a week before, passed him unheedingly; all save one, who eyed him for a moment, said "Poor devil!" in an undertone, and dropped a silber-gro' into his maimed hand. He felt glad of even this lame sympathy in his lowness; but most of all he prized the moistened glance of pity that flashed upon him from the great dark eyes of a lovely girl who passed him now and then as he slouched along. Once, a being as degraded and scurvy as his own outward self, turned to him, called him "*Dutzbruder*," asked him how he left them all in Berlin, stared at Ronald's blank look of non-recognition, and passed on with a muttered curse on his own stupidity in mistaking a stranger, in broad daylight, for his crony Kraut.

Another memory was of the strange lassitude that seemed to almost paralyze him after even moderate exertion, and caused him to drop exhausted on a bench on the terrace. when he had shuffled over less than half its length. More than once the suspicion crept upon him that only a portion of his vitality now remained to him, and that its greater part lay mysteriously coiled in Herr Lebensfunke's life-magnet. And this, in turn, broadened into a doubting distrust of the Herr himself—a dread lest the old man might in some way appropriate this stock of life to his own use, and so renew his fast-expiring lease for a score or two of years to come. At last this dread grew so painfully definite, that he hurried back to Freiberg a day before his appointed time, and once more found his twofold self wandering through its devious streets.

It was long after dark, and a thin rain slanted on the slippery stones, as he again made his way through the deserted and sleepy paths of the town to the old philosopher's house. He was wet, chilled, weary, and sick enough at heart as he leaned against the cold stone doorway and waited for an answer to his knock. The plash of the heavier rain-drops from the tiled caves was the only sound he heard for many minutes, until, at last, pattering feet neared him on the inside, and a child's voice asked who was there. To his friendly response the door was opened half-wide, and Vögelein's blank, pretty face peeped through.

Was Herr Lebensfunke at home? No; he had said that he wasn't at home: but then, she thought he was in the long room where mamma went to sleep. Could he be seen? No, she thought not; he was very tired, and, in her own—Vögelein's—opinion, he was going to sleep too, just as mamma did. And the wizened little face, with its eldritch eyes and tangled hair, was withdrawn, and the door began to close. Ronald forced himself inside, and grasped the child's arm.

"Vögelein, don't you know me?"

The girl, in nowise startled, gravely set her flickering candle on the doorstep, looked up at him wonderingly, as if he were an exhibition, and said she thought not, unless he had been asleep on the table.

"Good heavens!" cried Ronald, "can this child talk of nothing but people asleep on a table?"

But, as he spoke, a thought whirred through his brain. He drew the poor half-witted thing close to him and asked:

"Can Vögelein tell me something about mamma, and how she went to sleep?"

The child rambled on, pleased to find a listener to her foolish prattle. All he could connect into a narrative was that the girl's mother, some seven or eight years before, had been drained of her life by the awful magnet, and that, as the child said, "the Herr Doctor ever since had talked just like mamma."

His dread was well founded, then. The old man's one dream and aim was to prolong his wretched life; could he doubt that he would not now make use of the means he had so unwisely thrown in his way? He turned about, half maddened.

"Girl!" he cried, "I must see the old man! Where is he?"

He couldn't see him, she whined. He was asleep up there, on the table. At one o'clock he had said he would wake up.

He pushed past her, mounted to the long room, pressed open the unfastened door, and entered.

The old man and the corpse of his former self lay together under the light of a lamp that swung from the beam overhead. An insulated carbon point was directed to each white, still breast. From the old man's hand a cord ran to a key beyond, arranged to make or break connection at a touch. By it stood a clock, with a simple mechanism attached that bore upon a second key like the first, evidently planned to press upon it when the hands should mark a given hour. The child had said that he would wake at one, and it was now past midnight.

Ronald Wyde comprehended it all now. The wily old man's feeble life had been withdrawn into the great magnet, and mixed therein with what remained of his own. In less than an hour the key would fall, and the double stream would flow into and animate his young body, which would then wake to renewed life; while the cast-off shell beside it, worn to utter uselessness by a toilsome century, would be left to moulder as a mothed garment.

Surely no time was to be lost; his life depended upon instant action. And yet, comprehending this, he went to work slowly, and as a somnambulist might, acting almost by instinct, and well knowing that a blunder now meant irrevocable death.

Carefully disengaging the cord from the old man's yet warm grasp, and setting the carbon point aside, he lifted the shrivelled corpse and bore it away, to cast it on the white rubbish-heap in one corner. Returning to his work, he stripped himself, and laid down in the old man's place. As he did so, the distant Minster bells rang the three quarters.

Was there yet time?

He braced his shoulders firmly against the brass plate under them, and moved the carbon point steadily back to its place, with its tip resting on his breast; the silk-wrapped wire that dangled between it and the magnet quivering, as he did so, as with conscious life. Drawing a long breath, he tightened the cord, and heard a faint click as the key snapped down.

The same sharp sting as before instantly pricked his breast, tingling thrills pulsed over him, beats of light and shadow swept before his eyes, and he lost all consciousness. For how long he knew not. At last he felt, rather than saw, the lamp-rays flickering above him, and opened his eyes as though waking from a tired sleep. Sitting up, he gave a fearful look around him, as if dreading what he might see. The drunkard's body lay stretched and motionless beside him, and the clock marked three. He was saved!

Slipping down from his perilous bed, he resumed the old familiar garments that belonged to him as Ronald Wyde, shuddering with emotion as he did so. Only pausing to give one look at the pale heap in the shadowy corner, and at the other sleeper under the now dying lamp, he quitted the room and locked its heavy door upon the two silent guardians of its life-secrets. When he reached the street, he found the rain had ceased to drop, and that the cold stars blinked over the slumberous town.

Before noon he had taken leave of Frau Spritzkrapfen, turned buxom Lottchen scarlet all over by a hearty, sudden farewell-kiss, and was far on his way from Freiberg, with its red-vined balcony and its dark laboratory, never again to visit it or them. And as the busy engine toiled and shrieked, and with each beat of its mighty steam-heat carried him further away, his thoughts flew back and clustered around witless, brown-eyed birdling. Poor child, he never learned her fate.

    * * * * *

I heard this strange story from its hero, one sunny summer morning as we swept over the meadowy reaches of the Erie Railway, or hung along the cliff-side by the wooded windings of the Susquehanna. When he had ended it, he smiled languidly, and, showing me his still-mutilated hand, said that the old doctor's job had been a sad bungle, after all. In fact, the only physical-proof that remained to verify his story, was a curved blue spot where the ingoing current from the magnet had carried particles from the carbon point and lodged them beneath the skin. Psychologically, he was sadly mixed up, he said; for, since that time, he had felt that four lives were joined in him— his own, the remnant of Herr Lebensfunke's miserable hoard merged in that of poor birdling's mother, and, last of all, Hans Kraut's.

He left the cars soon afterward at Binghampton, watchfully followed by a stout, shabby man with a three days' beard stubbling his chin, who had occupied the seat in front of us, and had turned now and then to listen for a moment to Ronald's narration.

A week later, and I heard that he was dead—having committed suicide in a fit of delirium soon after his admission to the Binghampton Inebriate Asylum. The attendant who made him ready for burial noticed a singular blue mark on his left breast, that looked, he said, a little like a horse-shoe magnet.

Gallagher, Spelled Golyer

[In this manuscript fragment the "Golyers" make another appearance in John Hay's writing, figuring prominently in "The Blood Seedling" and in the Pike County ballads.]

There is a house in a Southern Capital looking on one of the prettiest squares in the world, where on almost any evening in the year, you will find a company of half a dozen men, and sometimes one or two women, setting before a fire which always glows and never smokes. I cannot say so much for the men, nor even for the women. There seems but one qualification required of the male visitors of this hospitable house, that they shall have something to say for themselves; and but one for the ladies, that they shall be good to look at. The purpose for which they gather there is not politics or primarily, flirtation; which differentiates this house from others in the city; the business of the place and hour is conversation. On most evenings, there is a brisk play of give and take: but sometimes, when the party is small and sympathetic, one guest may be drawn out to tell at considerable length of some passage in his life, while all the rest listen, or look at the glowing embers, in silence which amounts to the same thing as attention: but the evenings we most value and remember are those when the host, who usually passes the evening in blowing clouds of nicotine up the chimney, takes the conversation in hand and does the talking himself. There is one drawback to these apparently frank deliverances of his: he never talks about himself, but always of much less interesting people: nevertheless, there is a kind of documentary interest about his stories of the people he has met in the world's byways and some of them I have written out on returning home. This is one of them.

I have been thinking, he said—this remark was addressed to me—we were in *tout petit comité*—the hour was late and only two or three lingered about the fire—I have been thinking of the remark you made at dinner that there were only two careers in life in which success was certain—one, founding a new religion, and the other, getting into society. I have no experience in faith-founding, but, of course, after Joe Smith and Blavatzky, your remark is a truism, on that side of it. On the other I imagine it is equally true. We have all dined this week with people we swore last year we never would know. It is a stupid thing to say. "We must draw the line somewhere." Draw it where you please, it will no more stop travel than the meridian of Greenwich. The people who make up their minds to know you will do it, if you are worth their while, or if they think you are—which amounts to the same.

"But"—a smoker interrupted—"it certainly requires some means—some resources of purse, or brains or manners, to get and hold a place in society."

"It requires nothing," replied the Host, "except a cheek of bronze, and the heart of a Snob." If you are ready to face any amount of snubbing, and if you honestly love and worship rank and fashion with your whole heart, you will succeed, in spite of "the twin jailors of the daring heart, low birth and iron fortune." Of course it is far easier to take your seat among the Smart if you have a lot of money. With a good house, good wine, good horses, any place you want is at your disposition. The horse is the first title of nobility. The big house is of itself the seat of a Family. The full purse made originally all the Princes that now swagger in Italian cities. But when you have these, there is no merit in being fashionable. You buy your box ticket which gives you the run of the place—you don't earn it. But I have several cases in mind where I have seen the most unpromising circumstances lead to brilliant success—if you call it success to come to know people of rank and title.

"I read the other day in a newspaper of the death of a man in Syracuse, who in his chosen walk of life was as successful as Gladstone or Vanderbilt in theirs. I lived in Syracuse when I was a boy. We used to get our horses and buggies of an old fellow named Gallagher. He spelled his patronymic Golyer because he said it was pronounced so and it saved time and trouble. He had a shockheaded boy who helped him about the stable, held our horses when we started and took the reins when we returned. He was a serviceable well-meaning chap, and deserved the quarters the boys used to toss him after a buggy drive or sleigh-ride. His only fault was that he was not always on hand when he was wanted. But his father knew his habits: and a loud malediction sometimes accompanied in its flight by a brickbat would generally fetch young Golyer out from some shady corner of the stable yard. He would come not very briskly up with a crumpled story-paper in his hand and a look as of another world in his pale blue eyes. "There! jest look at that Image!" old Golyer would say. "A musin' and ablinkin' like an everlastin' bat! Well, Mark, how is Lord Alphonsus and Lady Victoriana Jane a getting' along by this time?"

These allusions to Quintillian's literary tastes would always bring the brick dust color to the youth's cheeks, but he would make no reply. There was no special malice in the old man's allusions. He was himself rather proud of his son's liking for what he considered genteel literature.

He was so quick to act on a hint that at last I became shy of giving them to him. One day he spoke in my presence disrespectfully of a friend of mine who had a papal title of nobility. "He calls himself Duke of Cluny just as if he was a real Duke like Launes or Bassano?"

"Beware, Golyer, how you make such distinctions," I answered. "Do you call a Corsican adventurer a greater authority than the Pope? Those titles you speak of so slightingly are derived from a Power only one remove from the Great White Throne."

I said this with a perfectly straight face and he almost trembled as he listened. "Well, by Jackson," he said, in an awe stricken voice, "I never thought of that."

About the Author

John Milton Hay (1838–1905) was best known as a statesman and public servant. He was private secretary and assistant to Abraham Lincoln, Ambassador to the Court of St. James (England), and Secretary of State under Presidents McKinley and Theodore Roosevelt, known for creating the 'Open Door" policy with China and for negotiating the construction of the Panama Canal. He was also a well-known writer whose works include the ten-volume *Abraham Lincoln: A History* (1890), co-authored with John Nicolay, for many years the standard Lincoln biography; *Castilian Days* (1871), a collection of essays about Spain; *Pike County Ballads*, local-color poetry set in the rural Illinois of his youth (1871); *The Bread-winners* (1883), a novel, and a number of short stories and poems.

About the Editor

George Monteiro is Professor Emeritus at Brown University. He maintains interests in the areas of English-language and Portuguese-language literature and culture. In addition to *Henry James and John Hay: The Record of a Friendship* and *The John Hay–Howells Letters,* he has published critical books on Henry James, Stephen Crane, Ernest Hemingway, Robert Frost, Elizabeth Bishop, Luis de Camões, and Fernando Pessoa. He has written numerous critical articles on American and Portuguese literature as well as four volumes of poetry and several translations of Portuguese poetry.

www.ingramcontent.com/pod-product-compliance
Lightning Source LLC
Chambersburg PA
CBHW020603180626
46810CB00007B/2623